Rings On Her Fingers

ReGina Welling

Rings on Her Fingers

ISBN-978-1-953044-95-2

Cover art by: L. Vryhof

www.reginawelling.com

First Edition
Printed in the U.S.A.

Contents

Chapter One

"Come in." A voice called through the curtain. "Enter and let us speak of the unknown."

Julie Hayward felt absolutely foolish. It was just like her outlandish best friend to think a visit to a psychic was a good engagement gift. Eloise Roman, who now called herself Gustavia, had a macabre sense of humor. Knowing Julie would be skeptical and embarrassed had done nothing to stop Gustavia dragging her in here. In fact, the more Julie protested, the more delighted her friend became.

"I promise you won't be disappointed," she whispered. "I've known her for years, and she's the real thing. She has incredible insight, and her readings are always helpful."

With a mental sigh indicating both dread and doubt, she followed Gustavia through the beaded curtain.

"Sit...please, sit." The smiling woman whose slightly round face was framed by dark hair simply pulled back in a ponytail and tied with a colorful silk scarf was not at all the type of person Julie had been expecting to meet. She wore no turban, no cape, and was bare of jewelry. No rings. No amulets. Nothing. Her voice was soft without any trace of the expected fake-sounding accent. She was just an attractive, normal-looking woman in her mid-twenties. Oddly, Julie felt both reassured and let down at the same time.

Gustavia, in her lacy white blouse, long batik skirt, and toe-ringed feet encased in chunky sandals came a lot closer to fulfilling Julie's expected vision of what a psychic medium might look like. Around Gustavia's neck, long strings of quartz crystals in a variety of colors with tiny bells and amulets hung nearly to her waist. When she walked, a musical tinkle arose from her person. Her soft brown eyes, outlined with Kohl, always seemed focused on a plane other than the earthly one. More crystals and beads were woven into the looping braids of her hair. She would have been completely disgusted to know Julie had bought into some media-driven stereotype, even for a moment.

She was not led into a dark room made atmospheric with suffocating clouds of incense; instead, there was only a faint smell of lavender in the air in the brightly lit dining room, where the sun streamed through a large bay window. Behind the table where the psychic sat was a large cabinet with elaborately carved doors; the door on the left hung open to reveal a nice tea set in a floral pattern. On the shelf below, within easy reaching distance, were two square bundles wrapped in velvet—Julie thought they probably held Tarot cards—and next to those was a small drawstring bag. It too was made of velvet.

On the way in, Julie had read the sign on the door outside **Madame Zephyr, Psychic Readings**. It hadn't inspired any confidence, what kind of name was **Zephyr**?

Gustavia said, "Julie, I would like you to meet my friend, Kathleen."

"Call me Kat." The woman smiled and held out a hand. "Welcome."

"Nice to meet you," Julie said automatically, then asked, "Kat? Who's Madame Zephyr, then?"

"Zephyr was my grandmother's professional name, and I thought it would be nice to carry on the tradition."

As she shrugged then sat down, Julie's eyes were drawn to Kat's. They were a deep, velvety blue, but the expression in them was completely vacant. She was puzzled until she realized Kat was blind. A blind psychic. How did she read Tarot cards? Did those things come in Braille? She hoped

Gustavia had not paid too much for this visit. Immediately, Julie regretted the snarky thought; she was not normally prone to that type of rudeness, but the whole idea of psychics and Tarot cards and whatever else might happen had her a bit freaked out.

"What kind of reading would you like?" asked Kat.

"Any kind is fine," Julie replied, trepidation obvious in her voice.

The psychic reached for a deck of Tarot cards and began to shuffle them expertly. Then she handed the deck to Julie. "Shuffle until your intuition tells you to stop, then cut the cards with your left hand," she said. Julie did as she was told then handed the deck back to Kat who laid out ten cards in a pattern on the table. Six cards formed a cross with four cards stacked vertically beside it.

"This is the Celtic Cross spread. It will help define your current path and indicate where that path will lead if you continue on it."

Julie just nodded, forgetting Kat could not see her. She looked closely at the cards and saw, yes, they were indeed marked in Braille.

Instead of touching the cards to read them, Kat sat unmoving, and then her head fell forward onto her chest. Julie began to shift in her chair. Now, what? With no idea what to expect next, she cast an exasperated glance at Gustavia who shrugged; she also seemed surprised by this turn of events. Feeling more and more uncomfortable, Julie had just about decided to get up and leave when Kat raised her head. Something was different, but Julie couldn't quite put her finger on it. Then a slow chill began to crawl up her spine. The eyes gazing into hers were no longer deeply blue and vacant. They were lighter, an icy gray color, and it was obvious their owner could see her clearly. These eyes knew Julie, and she them as they began to drink in every detail of her appearance.

Slowly, Kat's features seemed to shift. The angles and planes melted then multiplied like a double exposure in a photograph so that overlying the medium's face was one Julie would have known anywhere.

Rooted to the spot, Julie just stared, then her heart skipped a beat before it began to pound in her chest. All the blood drained from her face, leaving her normally rosy skin a ghostly white beneath its liberal dusting of freckles. She slumped in the chair feeling slightly faint, her hand pressed to her forehead. After a long moment had passed, Kat spoke in voice Julie never expected to hear again in this world.

"Oh, my darling girl; it is so good to see you." Kat held out both of her hands. Only a second passed before Julie reached out her own trembling hands and allowed them to be held in a warm grasp. Tears slipped unheeded down her face.

"Grams... is that really you?" Julie whispered.

"Yes, lovely one. It is me."

"I've missed you so much, but how— what is happening?"

"I know; I have missed you as well," Kat replied in Gram's voice, "But I've been with you every day. Now listen closely: there is something you need to know, and a job for you to do. "

"What? A job; are you telling me you have unfinished business? What do you mean?" Julie asked.

As eerily as it had appeared, the image of Julie's grandmother faded, almost like melting wax, then reformed into another, less familiar face. It was one Julie recognized, but she couldn't quite remember from where.

"I'll tell you what it is," said a new voice, a man's voice. "This is your great-grandfather. Start with the magic garden. That's where it begins. The key will show you the first clue; it will lead you to the rest. You're not a fool like your grandfather was; remember my last words. Start with the magic garden." Now Julie knew where she had

12

seen that face: in the painting above the fireplace in the home she had once shared with her grandmother, the home that was now her sole responsibility.

What did he just say? The air seemed thick as molasses as it took several moments for her thoughts to clear and allow the words to sink in.

Julie shook her head in amazement. This was not happening. Magic garden. Her great-grandfather. What did it all mean? She looked helplessly at Gustavia who, for once, had nothing to say.

Before she had time to ask, Kat's head fell forward again. It stayed that way for several minutes. When she lifted her chin, her eyes were once again deep blue and vacant; her face, if possible, had even less color in it than Julie's.

Looking from one friend to the other, Gustavia quickly realized this was not a usual experience for Kat and that Julie was now shaking violently. She switched into caretaker mode getting them all a soothing cup of tea and respecting the silence both women seemed to need to regain their composure.

After several minutes, the silence started feeling awkward, so Gustavia tentatively spoke, "Well, that was ..." she trailed off as Julie quelled her with a look; clearly she was still too upset to discuss what had happened. She turned to Kat.

"Are you alright? Is there something I can do?" Kat shook her head, no.

Even more awkward minutes passed.

Kat continued to sit in contemplative silence until, not knowing what else to do, Gustavia guided her still-shaken friend out the door saying quietly to the psychic, "I'll call you later."

The car ride home was mostly silent with Julie ignoring her friend's frequent sidelong glances. Gustavia squirmed in the seat. Several times she opened her mouth to speak; but, for once, seemed reluctant to begin a conversation and finally subsided.

Once home, Julie gently, but firmly, closed the door in Gustavia's face and went inside. Over the living room fireplace hung the large, beautifully painted portrait of Julius Hayward, Julie's great-grandfather, the man she had been named after. She stood in front of it for a long time thinking about what had just happened, trying to make sense of it and worrying a little about what was to come.

Julius Hayward had considered himself a mechanical mastermind, inventing some indispensable component used by the military. Rumor had it he had made a small fortune. He

16

used some of the money to remodel the house then built a large workshop. Over the following years, he conceived dozens of strange, unsellable inventions still found on display in the old workshop. Grams had turned it into a free museum that hardly anyone ever visited. She said he had been ahead of his time, a forward thinker, but eventually, these worthless contraptions had eaten his entire net worth.

His only other successful invention had been some small widget used in aircraft for which Grams, and now Julie still received the occasional royalty check. Julius had been an eccentric man. Secretive about his work and about his finances, when he died at the relatively young age of 52 it appeared that the balance of his fortune was gone, along with the family silver and all of the jewelry passed down to him by his mother. His will hinted at more— at there being plenty of money to take care of the house and his family, but other than a trust to pay the taxes, nothing more was ever found.

Unable to quiet her thoughts, the day's events replayed in Julie's mind spurring an internal argument over whether it had all been an elaborate hoax or if she'd truly spoken to her beloved grandmother. If it was a hoax, it was beyond cruel; if it was meant as a joke, it had failed miserably to be funny. If she'd been the one behind it, Gustavia couldn't help knowing this would be intensely painful to Julie who was still grieving her grandmother's loss.

Aside from the shock of hearing Grams voice again, there was this magic garden business. She vaguely remembered something about the phrase—but she couldn't quite pull it to the front of her mind—or maybe she had read it in a book. The phrase seemed familiar. Or was she thinking of **The Secret Garden**? Her thoughts continued to whirl, and she could not get them to settle. This was ridiculous.

Yet, the idea there might actually be something of value hidden away somewhere, something valuable enough to cover the cost of repairing the old house, was intriguing. She couldn't help thinking how wonderful it would be if it were true. The house had an interesting history and great bones; it would be a wonderful place to raise a family.

Not long out of college, with a degree in Art History she'd barely had the chance to use, Julie was alone in the great big home she had inherited. She still had a little bit of the money from her parents' insurance policy left in her savings account. The taxes were paid by her great-grandfather's trust;

but when Grandpa James had fallen ill, it had wiped out the largest part of the nest egg Grams had managed to save. Her own illness had used most of the rest; and, when she died, she'd left her granddaughter a large house in need of some costly repairs. Thankfully there was no mortgage on the place; but, while Julie made a modest income selling her photographs through a local gallery, the needed repairs were well beyond her means. In recent months, she and Gustavia—who turned out to be handy with a hammer—had done some judicious patching, enough to buy her a few more months to come up with some funds.

She knew it wouldn't be long before she would have to make a decision to either sell the house or think of something to do with it to generate enough income to keep it. Maybe she could open a bed and breakfast and become a total cliché. Sometimes, she thought she might turn it into a sort of artist's retreat or even offer it to some film companies for location shooting. Most of the ideas she came up with, though, required a certain amount of capital be spent on fixing up the place before she could test the possibilities. It would be a gamble, and Julie was not much of a gambler. Life had taught her to be practical.

Logan Ellis, Julie's fiancé, had his own opinions and was not shy about airing them. He was constantly saying there was no need for them to own a house this big, her work would sell better in the city, his work was there, the house was too much for them, and she should let it go now while it still had some value. If they began doing the repairs it needed, they would never get a good return on the investment. He thought the place was a money pit and didn't understand how Julie could be so attached to her home.

If any of this business about hidden wealth were true, Julie figured convincing Logan would be a hard sell.

Confessing she had gotten her information from a pair of dead relatives by way of a psychic, well, that was information that seemed better left unsaid. Especially since she wasn't sure she believed any of this improbable story herself. As her fear and confusion began to fade, Julie became aware of anger hiding underneath all of those other emotions. More specifically, she was angry at her best friend.

Gustavia had dragged her into this situation, and there was no way this was going to end quickly or well. This was the type of thing that Gustavia lived. For once that woman committed herself to a thing, she followed through, no matter what. It was one of the traits

Julie most loved about her, but also one that sometimes caused an unbelievable amount of annoyance. It was both a blessing and a curse.

The more she thought about her friend and this mess, the angrier Julie became. The whole thing was ridiculous. If there had been any hidden family treasure, surely someone would have found it by now. If this was Gustavia's idea of a prank, she had a twisted sense of humor. None of this was funny. How had the so-called psychic nailed Gram's voice so perfectly, though? This wasn't like Gustavia; she had never been a malicious person. Maybe that psychic had talked her into something. But why? Julie couldn't see where either of them had anything to gain in this situation.

Chapter Two

Taking a cup of tea out the back door and forcing herself to relax on the porch swing, Julie began to calm her chaotic thoughts with an effort of will. She needed to put her feelings of anger aside and look at this thing logically; even if the very idea of applying logical thought to this situation told her just how far down the rabbit hole she already was, and it looked like this might be just the beginning.

Determined to put the whole incident out of her mind, Julie spent the rest of the evening Photoshopping a few of her latest batch of images. When Logan called, she rushed him off the phone with a promise to see him the next day. He was one more complication in an already stressful day.

Tossing and turning her way through a restless night, she woke up with the same unresolved feelings she'd had at bedtime. When the phone rang during breakfast, Julie, thinking it might be Gustavia, ignored the caller ID and did not bother to answer. Then, when it rang again fifteen minutes later—and then every fifteen minutes for the next two hours—she was sure she'd been right. Finally, the ringing stopped. Julie sighed with relief and helped herself to another cup of tea. She'd barely managed to drink half of it when she spotted an all too familiar car pulling up the drive.

Gustavia rang the doorbell once, twice, and then pounded on the door.

"C'mon, open up! I know you're in there, and I'm not leaving," she called, her voice muffled by the heavy wooden door. "I have a key and you know I'll use it."

Reluctantly, but knowing it would be fruitless to ignore Gustavia--persistence was one of her more obvious qualities-- Julie let her in.

Gustavia flew through the door, long skirts swirling around her ankles, and hugged Julie hard.

"What's with the full media blackout?"

Julie started to answer, "I ... yesterday ... I ..."

"Wasn't she great? I told you she was the real thing. Where do you think the magic garden is? I couldn't sleep all night wondering if you'd figured it out," Gustavia said, following her into the kitchen. She reminded Julie of a puppy begging to be played with, even down to the way she moved. If she'd been born with a tail, it would have been of the thin, wiry variety that constantly wagged in circles.

Stepping back, Gustavia looked at her friend and quickly perceived something was wrong. It didn't take a lot of intuition to see it; Julie was annoyed, but along with the annoyance was a healthy dose of fear. That was understandable; it wasn't every day a person had a conversation with a pair of dead relatives. That kind of thing was bound to stir up a few strong emotions, especially in those who didn't readily believe in the supernatural. In an attempt to lighten the mood,

Gustavia did a butt-shaking dance around the room chanting, "There's magic in the garden," while Julie stared at her with a raised eyebrow, poured out her now-cold tea and busied herself brewing a new pot.

Sighing and trying to stay annoyed, Julie replied, "There is no magic garden. After I had some time to think about it, I remembered hearing stories of how my grandfather dug up most of the property while he was alive; and, clearly, he never found a thing."

"Well there has to be one, your great grandfather said there was," Gustavia stopped dancing.

"Oh, Gustavia, you don't actually believe that was my great-grandfather, do you?" Julie rolled her eyes, scorn evident in the tone of her voice. Gustavia grabbed a mug from the cupboard, then the two women seated themselves at one end of the old trestle table while Julie poured them both a cup of tea. Looking at her friend over the rim of a favorite, daisy-covered mug, Julie realized Gustavia did, indeed, believe that very thing.

"Don't you?" Gustavia replied, then she looked at Julie. "No, I can see you don't." Then, taking another long look, her eyes widened, then her gaze turned speculative. She tilted her head first left, then right, and squinted. "Your aura is rumpled. I've never seen it do that before. I wonder what it means."

"It probably means I should have hung it up to dry instead of leaving it in a heap on the bathroom floor," was the sarcastic reply.

"Very funny, but this is serious," Gustavia jumped up and grabbed Julie's arm, "Come on, we have to go see Ammie."

"Who?"

"Ammie--Amethyst. She does the most amazing work with damaged auras." Gustavia had already pulled Julie halfway to the front door. When Gustavia set her mind on something, stopping her was like trying to stop a steamroller: a steamroller painted

34

purple and hung all over with crystals. She shook the thought away; and, before she knew it, she was in the car and on the way to whatever new age habitat someone named Amethyst might frequent.

Riding in Gustavia's car was an experience in itself. When she'd bought the 1977 Maverick from the proverbial little old lady, it only had 18,000 miles on it. The car had been immaculate: rust-colored, but rust-free. Bought at the beginning of her new age transformation, Gustavia claimed her car had a calming aura and just reeked of beneficial energy.

She had sewn herself a set of seat covers out of a nubby chenille bedspread dyed in rainbow colors. Next, she'd removed the original headliner, reupholstered it with fabric in a moon and stars pattern, then pinned a grid of wire-wrapped crystals over the whole thing. Parts of the doors and dashboard had been covered in tan vinyl leaving a fair bit of exposed body-colored metal which Gustavia had hand-painted with designs of all types from Celtic to Japanese calligraphy.

But the topper was the figurine she'd mounted on the dashboard. In a local junk shop, Gustavia had found one of the old hula dancing dolls, the kind with a grass skirt that swayed with the motion of the car. She had redressed it in a gypsy outfit and then fitted it out with a pair of angel wings.

New age music competed with the **tinkling** of the tiny bells hung on strings from the mirror as Gustavia drove with her usual abandon.

"How many speeding tickets have you had?" Julie asked dryly.

"I never drive faster than my angels can fly," was the smug reply; and, while not exactly feeling safe, Julie envied her friend that complete trust in the universe. Losing the last of her small family had left Julie bereft and lonely. Thankfully, though she'd also been grieving the loss, Gustavia had realized how much she had been needed, and for the first few weeks after Gram's death, had stayed at the house and helped make all of the arrangements. Julie knew she could count on her friend; they shared a sisterly bond. If that bond required temporarily putting the irritation aside and going along to see someone who claimed to be an aura reader, then so be it.

"Is Amethyst a new friend of yours?" Julie tried to get some idea what might happen next.

"You know her; I think the two of you met at my lunar eclipse party. She changes her name every year; she's working her way through the chakra colors. Last year her name was Jade."

"Is she the one who wore the elf ears?"

"No, that was Mishka; and those were her real ears. Well--at least after the surgery," Gustavia replied. Julie raised one eyebrow; but, deciding not to probe further looked out the window.

"Oh, what are we stopping here for?" Julie asked as Gustavia pulled into a small field bordered by forest. The center of the field swelled into a low hill then fell away toward a lovely view of the lake.

"This is where Amethyst lives."

"Where, in a tree?" Julie shifted in her seat, looking around to see if she was missing something, sarcasm evident in her tone.

"No, silly. Follow me." Gustavia indicated a well-worn path in the grass that led around the gently rising mound of earth. On the other side, set into the hill, were large windows and a beautifully decorated door. Amethyst lived underground. Oh, maybe she's a hobbit, Julie thought but didn't bother to voice the sentiment. Instead, she heaved a mental sigh and wondered what fresh hell she was about to walk into.

Gustavia knocked on the intricately carved door and waited only a few seconds before throwing it open and calling out, "Hey, Ammie, are you here? It's Gustavia and Julie."

As she walked around the corner, Julie recognized Amethyst immediately. Her hair and eyebrows were dyed a delicate shade of lavender, as were her clothes. Flowing chiffon seemed draped on her slight frame as if it were a purple cloud that had just drifted down and decided to clothe her. She also remembered at their last meeting, Amethyst, whose name had been Jade at the time, sported a lovely sage green as her signature color.

Amethyst wafted over and kissed Gustavia on both cheeks.

"So good to see you." She said, her voice surprisingly deep and substantial for such a wraith of a woman.

"Do you remember my friend Julie?" Gustavia asked.

"Why, of course." And Amethyst moved forward then tilted her head in much the same way Gustavia had earlier and circled Julie slowly. "Oh, my, your aura is rumpled."

"So I've been told," Julie replied dryly wondering if **rumpled** was a technical term. "What's the diagnosis?"

Stroking her chin, head still tilted, Amethyst circled Julie. Then she began plucking the air around the woman's body as though removing unwanted particles and flicking them away. Julie stood helplessly, caught somewhere between laughter and tears over the absurdity of this; but, as the plucking continued, she actually began to feel emotionally lighter.

This went on for several minutes until finally, Amethyst stopped.

"Have you had contact with the spirit world recently?" She asked.

Julie was reluctant to answer. It occurred to her how this could just be another phase of the prank.

Gustavia answered for Julie, "Yes, she has. She saw Kat yesterday, and her grandmother and great-grandfather came through. I think it scared her. In fact, I think it scared Kat, too."

"No. I don't think so." Julie said loudly, finally reaching the end of her rope, "I don't believe in all that mumbo jumbo. It is just a huge, cruel joke; and I think you're all in on it."

"Oh, Jules!" Gustavia cried, her eyes bright with tears, going to her friend, she hugged her. "I would never do that to you. How could you ever think I would? This is all just going too fast for you, I understand."

"No, I don't think you do. I feel all churned up; half of me wants to believe what happened, and the other half is scared to death that it did."

"Nevertheless," Amethyst chimed in gently, "we should repair the damage to your aura. Let's have a cup of tea while I come up with a plan." This did nothing to settle Julie's nerves, and she thought she'd already had enough tea for one day. She just wanted this day— no this entire week—to be over with, and quickly.

As Amethyst led the way deeper into her underground home, Julie got a chance to take a good look around at the cozy residence that had been carved out of the hill. The walls were stucco painstakingly hand-textured and painted to resemble sandstone. Deep shadows curved into horizontal bands shading from mahogany to palest orange. Small up-lights placed at intervals along the walls highlighted the undulating patterns. It truly was breathtaking. Leading out the back of the large front room was a short hallway. An open door on the left led to a spacious bedroom. The door on the right revealed a small bathroom, and just past that, a large archway framed the kitchen. Though not as dramatically lit as the living room, the room was cozy with highly polished cabinets lining the walls above a granite counter top. Tube-shaped skylights that had not been visible from the other side of the hill let bright sunlight into the room.

Amethyst busied in the kitchen, while Julie and Gustavia sat down at the table. In just a few short minutes, the tea was ready; and by the time they were finished drinking it, Julie felt steadier, more balanced.

After a lengthy discussion containing strange phrases—one Julie gave up trying to follow—over what to do for the rumpled aura, the two new-agers decided a guided meditation was the best option. Once the decision was made, they moved quickly to install Julie comfortably on a pile of pillows in the front room, put in a CD of soothing music, settled in beside her.

In a calming voice, Amethyst directed Julie to relax and concentrate on her breathing. Then she asked Julie to picture herself walking through a sunlit meadow with fragrant grasses and flowers slowly fluttering in a warm breeze.

Not bothering to try and imagine any such thing, the meditating, instead, gave Julie time to think objectively. Gustavia had been unfailingly helpful during the first few weeks following Gram's death: she'd made it a priority to take care of her friend and share the grieving process. From the first time Julie had brought her college roommate home, Grams had seen Gustavia's need for acceptance and family. Without a moment's hesitation, she'd opened her arms in welcome and won herself an honorary granddaughter. She was just that kind of person, and Gustavia had blossomed as a result of love and attention.

All three women shared a deep love of art. Gustavia made a nice living writing children's books, but she also had a passion for painting and creating mixed media art. She and Grams spent hours debating the nuances of technique and style. Whenever they got into their ongoing discussion about the definition of art vs. craft, you might as well leave the room. They could be at it for hours.

It just was not in Gustavia's nature to be deliberately hurtful. She might be eccentric; she might be outspoken, but she always meant well. Therefore, this was no prank. That thought was a sobering one. If this wasn't a joke, then Grams and great-grandfather had actually spoken to her. Through a psychic medium, no less. Following that line of reasoning, the magic garden might also be real. Goosebumps prickled up Julie's arms at the notion.

At just that second, both Gustavia and Amethyst cried out.

"Her aura, it just healed itself."

"Did you see that?"

"What did it?" Gustavia asked.

"I gave in to the inevitable," Julie grumbled. "If you weren't playing a prank on me, it must have been Grams speaking through the psychic."

Gustavia beamed. Amethyst beamed. Julie sighed. She was in for it now.

For the second day in a row, the two friends rode silently back to Hayward House, both lost in thought, both thinking of the magic garden and how to find it. Gustavia's plan of attack involved more psychic readings and dowsing, while Julie planned a conversation with the man who had written her family history. Failing that, a visit to the public library might turn up something new.

Again, she thought there was something familiar about the phrase **magic garden**, but Julie could not remember where she had seen it before; it was maddening.

Gustavia dropped Julie off and sat for a moment contemplating her next step. After deciding to begin with a return visit to Kat, she made a quick call on her cell phone, then rocketed down the drive in her usual fashion.

Chapter Three

After a warm greeting, Kat invited Gustavia to sit.

"So, yesterday was quite something; that was the first time I have ever heard you channel an actual spirit," Gustavia said.

"Between you and me, it was the first time it ever happened like that.

They just took over, and not being in control of my own body was scary. But, that's not all; something else happened; I couldn't believe it. Nothing like that ever happened before. That's not how it usually works." Kat rambled in a rush of nervousness.

Ever the soul of compassion, Gustavia reached out and squeezed her friend's hand. "Well, you handled it like a pro. Is it prying if I ask how it usually works?"

Kat hesitated.

"It's okay, really; you don't have to tell me. I know it's none of my business."

"It's not that. I'm afraid it will ruin the mystique. And I don't usually talk to my friends about this side of things. Most people don't believe."

"That sounds lonely," Gustavia said. "Tell me. You'll feel better, and I never judge; I promise."

"I wasn't always blind. It began shortly after I started seeing spirits or came into my powers or whatever you want to call it. I was scared and didn't want to see them anymore, and so I gradually lost my sight. My doctors think it's a form of hysterical blindness."

Gustavia gave Kat's hand another squeeze as she continued to speak.

"When I channeled Julie's family, I could see again," tears began to slide slowly down her face.

"Oh, Kat, that's wonderful and awful all at the same time."

"Yes. It means the doctors are right: I really am causing my own affliction, and I don't know what to do about it. What does that say about me?"

"It says you're scared and doctors don't always understand fear. Did they suggest therapy?"

"Yes; but after the first visit, I stopped going. The therapist didn't accept my abilities, which was pretty ridiculous considering his dead mother was in the room talking to me during the entire session."

Gustavia chuckled. "So can you see the spirits or do you just hear them?"

"Oh, I see them; they appear as dream figures, sort of like a memory. They are usually just misty shapes in the darkness. That is what freaked me out the other day; it was the first time in years I have seen anything besides blobs and darkness--and so clearly, too."

"So, now you are conflicted: you probably want to do it again, even if it's scary; and you're probably worried about what it means that it happened at all."

"Yes." Relief caused by unburdening herself to someone who understood finally allowed Kat's body to relax; she rotated shoulders sore from being held so stiffly. "That is exactly the problem, and you were totally right, I do feel better talking about it."

Gustavia went around the table and pulled Kat into a hug.

"Okay, enough of that. Let me do a reading for you," Kat said. It was obvious she was feeling much more comfortable now with the heavy emotional burden shared.

"Without Julie here, I can't give you the full picture; but we can still get some idea of what might happen, or at least the part you will play in what is to come," she explained while handing a

Tarot deck based on mythological stories to Gustavia to shuffle.

The first card drawn off the deck was The Fool; indicating there would be a new journey. This was not news to either of the women, so they quickly moved on to the second card in the layout which was laid crosswise over the first: the Crossing card, the five of cups.

"This card warns of a betrayal, usually in a romantic relationship. It comes from the story of Psyche and Eros: when Eros keeps his face hidden and asks Psyche to respect this decision, she agrees; but then, after he goes to sleep, she takes a peek. He

sees this as a betrayal and leaves her."
Kat turned her face with its unseeing
eyes toward Gustavia, "In this way,
both partners betray the other: one by
hiding something and the other by a
lack of trust. Does this make any sense
to you?"

Not wanting to speak ill of him, but
unable to help herself, Gustavia
hesitated briefly before answering,
"Since day one, I've thought something
about Julie's fiancé, Logan, was—well—
not on the up. It always feels like he
has a hidden agenda if that makes any
sense; but on the surface, he seems
devoted and caring.

Kat nodded.

"He doesn't like me; and, worse, he thinks I'm too stupid to realize it. The comments he makes seem harmless; he plays it off like he is teasing, but I feel the malice behind his words. I don't like him either, and I'm pretty sure he knows it."

Turning up the third, or Crowning card, revealed the High Priestess in her ethereal robes standing on a set of steps. Kat thought for a moment as she placed the card above the first two then said, "In this position, I think she represents you and your intuition. The Crowning card shows what is going on right now; your sensitivity to this situation caused you to bring Julie here to meet her grandparents. You need to continue to pay attention to your innermost feelings."

"Do you think this card also represents you? The spirits used you once, and I'd bet they'll do it again. There's no way you won't end up more involved in this."

"Maybe," Kat said thoughtfully as she turned over another card.

Gustavia had had enough Tarot readings to know what the next position in the layout meant: it represented the challenge at the heart of the problem. She watched Kat settle the card into place below the first two crossed cards: the Ace of Wands. "Does that mean what I think it does? That we

are at the beginning of an adventure?"
she asked.

"Yes, that is exactly what it means.
An adventure. Not just for Julie; but
also for you, since this reading is about
your connection in the events to come."

Kat continued, "The next two cards
show past and future influences. Let's
see what we have." She turned the
next two cards over rapidly placing one
on either side of the first two cards
forming a cross shape: Page of Swords
and Ace of Pentacles. "This is an
interesting combination, gossip and the
possibility of a legacy."

"Would the family legend qualify as gossip since we already know about the legacy part?" asked Gustavia.

"That would certainly fit. Now, the next two cards will show what your role should be." Kat turned over the next card placing it to the bottom right of the cards already on the table: Strength.

"Your strength will be needed, but there could also be a problem with pride, maybe something to do with your family. You will need to be watchful so that pride does not get in your way." She then laid the next card directly above Strength; this card was the King of Swords.

Kat touched the card to read its markings in Braille then tapped it with her finger. "You will find a time where it becomes necessary to take charge of the situation even when you fear you will be resented for doing so."

The next to last card in the layout would reveal Gustavia's hopes and fears, and the card that landed in this position, directly above the King of Swords, was the Lovers. Kat contemplated for a moment then said, "Well, this is unexpected."

"The Lovers often signifies a type of love triangle. In this case, there could be several explanations. Your relationship with Julie and Logan and your dislike of him might form a triangular relationship. Or, there may be another man who enters the picture. There may also be a combination of these two events."

Gustavia nodded; then, remembering Kat could not see the gesture, murmured her assent. After a moment, she quietly admitted one of her biggest fears was Logan poisoning Julie against her.

One last card was turned over to take its place above the Lovers. This card indicated the final outcome: it was the Ace of Swords, meaning there would be conflict and danger ahead. Neither woman was thrilled at seeing this card, though both were thankful for the warning it brought.

Gustavia was unusually sober as she and Kat discussed possible outcomes and actions she might need to take. Clearly, the situation had the potential to become serious. Neither of the women had a good feeling about Logan. Each felt he could be dangerous if provoked and there was a good chance he had ulterior motives.

"My spirit guide keeps showing me a badge, and I hear the word **call**. Does this mean anything to you?" Kat asked.

"Unfortunately, it does," Gustavia answered without enthusiasm. "That would be my brother, and calling him is the last thing I want to do."

"Well, you might be happy to know my guide is also saying **reconcile** and **family** so maybe this will be a step in the right direction."

Gustavia shrugged. "Reconciliation is not in my immediate plan; but if I must, I'll deal with it. Calling my brother is only an option if there is a real danger or something criminal is happening." Voluntarily spending time with any of her family was not high on Gustavia's list of priorities. Julie was her family now, and someday she hoped to start one of her own. Sooner rather than later, she thought.

"Is your guide telling you anything positive?" She asked.

"Yes, two distinct outcomes are possible: one ends badly, but the other with true happiness. Though either of the two paths led through danger. You and Julie must both be careful."

Chapter Four

Hayward House sat in shabby splendor on grounds that had been passed down through Julie's family. Its original architecture had relied heavily on Greek influence until Julie's eccentric great-grandfather, Julius, had altered the structure to bring in some Gothic elements: elements that included four beautifully elaborate stained glass windows. The two styles did not mesh particularly well but certainly created a house with unique character.

As Julie walked through the front door, she heard the phone ringing. She checked the Caller ID, saw Logan's number at his office, and thought it odd that he hadn't called her cell phone.

"Hi, Sweetie," she answered.

"Hey, Baby; how did it go with the whackadoo brigade?" He asked.

"That's not nice, but I have to say it was an interesting experience. You would've hated it," she decided not to share the story over the phone—it would be hard enough to believe in person—"are we still on for tonight?"

"No, it turns out I have an early meeting tomorrow, so I'm planning on turning in early tonight. Oh, and I made the appointment with the lawyer for 11 am tomorrow." Julie's lighthearted mood quickly turned to pique. What was it with people these last couple days? Everyone was pressuring her to do things she just did not want to do.

"Do we really need to do this? I mean, a prenup seems so cold-blooded. Don't you think we should at least be married before we start thinking about making wills and taking out life insurance policies?"

"Honey, you know I'm only doing this for your sake; after we are married, it will be my job to protect you and to take care of you."

"I have been doing just fine with taking care of myself for quite some time, Logan," she answered dryly.

There was a short pause. "Well, you know I only want the absolute best for you, and I wish you'd trust me to know what you need. I have to get back to work; see you tomorrow. Love you," Logan cut off the call before she could argue the point.

Julie hung up the phone and sighed. Thinking about dealing with the lawyer tomorrow was just one more stressful factor in an already stressful week. It was not a common occurrence for her to speak to dead relatives and have her rumpled aura repaired; but, for different reasons, the dread of having to deal with these legal matters was just as unsettling. She and Logan weren't even married yet, and she thought the whole thing was ridiculous.

Over the past few weeks Logan hadn't been himself, and lately she'd been getting the feeling there was something deeper behind his new attitude. He couched it under the guise of wanting to take care of her, but it just felt a bit off. Maybe he was suffering from work stress, but she had a fairly advanced BS meter, and he was beginning to ring that bell just a little. Okay, more than a little. She didn't like the feeling at all. He had always seemed so caring; but, lately, there had been an air of condescension centered around her decision-making ability that put her on edge.

Choosing lemonade over her habitual cup of tea, Julie wandered around the house thinking about the decidedly cool reception Logan had gotten from her grandmother.

When pressed, Grams had said there was nothing specifically unlikeable about the man, but she couldn't bring herself to like him. He wasn't warm enough. Since she preferred a relationship based more on respect than romance, Julie assumed it was just a sign on their different outlooks on marriage and nothing to worry about. Logan was supportive; and if he was a little too concerned over the legal and financial side of their marriage, maybe this wasn't a fault. Deeply respectful of the grandmother who had shown her such an infinite and unconditional amount of love, this was one time when Julie had not deferred to Gram's opinion. Maybe she should have paid more attention at the time.

Raised by people who would settle for nothing less than the drama of an epic romance, Julie liked to think she was more practical than that. She certainly wasn't about to give in to her romantic side or even to admit that it existed. If Logan was willing to deal with certain details, she could step back a bit and let him. That would be the practical thing to do, as long as his reasons were valid. But, lately, she'd come to realize that taking care of details was one thing; insinuating he had to do so because she wasn't capable of taking care of herself was another entirely, and this had become a bit of a theme over the past few weeks. Frankly, it pissed her off.

Julie topped off her glass and carried it outside to the formal garden. She always gained a level of serenity when she visited this part of the property.

The midmorning light fell softly through the trees and sparkled across dew-laden grass. Sitting on a bench just slightly warmed from the sun, Julie took a deep breath of air that carried the scent of carefully tended spring blossoms. She felt close to Grams here—in this place that had been her favorite—and with everything that had happened over the past few days, she needed that feeling. Grief still washed over her unexpectedly sometimes, taking away her breath and dumping her heart down into the pit of her stomach. This was one of those times.

Her eyes filled with tears as she relaxed into the wracking spasm of heartache, dropping her head into her hands. Julie didn't see the faint shimmer beside her on the bench, didn't feel the touch of the ghostly hand that brushed down her hair as it stirred in the faint breeze. She sobbed out her pain until spent, then just sat for a few moments pulling herself back together with an effort.

Grams and Grandpa James had made wonderful parents. They'd raised her together for five years until James had arisen one morning complaining of pain in his stomach. Three days later the doctor said he had cancer and, after just six short weeks, he was gone. From then on it was just Julie and her grandmother, Estelle, until last fall when, at age 89, her kidneys had failed. Grams had remained remarkably active right up until her final illness.

It was time to put these thoughts aside and concentrate on the mess that Gustavia had unwittingly dumped in her life. First, she needed to look for the copy of the family history she remembered having seen in the library and read through it to see if there was anything helpful to be learned.

With any luck, the book would tell her more about the deathbed story that had caused her grandfather to conduct a short but frantic search for buried treasure on the grounds. Julie had never paid it much attention because Grams had passed the story off as the fantasy of a dying man; but, taking recent events into account, there might be more to it. If there was money or something else of value hidden on the property, her most pressing financial problems would be solved.

Of course, that all depended on finding the magic garden if it existed at all; and Julie felt a little foolish at the very idea of looking for clues.

Two hours later, she sighed and gave up the search. The slim volume of family history was not in the library. Julie had not only spent time tearing the place apart and making an unholy mess besides; but she'd missed her lunch and, even worse, was now going to be late setting up for her afternoon photography client.

Chapter Five

Since she was running late, Julie hurried into her studio to get everything ready. Product photography was not something she normally did; but Tamara, the jewelry maker who owned the shop next door to the gallery, had talked her into shooting fifty pieces to include in the jewelry shop's new Internet store.

During the initial consultation, the two women had decided to feature each piece against a background of neutral gray. Julie adjusted a spotlight to provide a strong, directional side light to add a bit of drama by bringing out the texture of the jewelry, then she installed a second, softer "fill" light at the front to create more depth and dimension. She then set up a tripod and fitted one camera with a standard lens and the other with a macro lens for extreme close up work.

Tamara, a freckle-faced redhead of indeterminate age, arrived promptly, breezing in with her small plastic tote full of carefully packed jewelry. She set down the tote, hugged Julie and exclaimed, "Finally, I get my chance to peek inside this house. My brother has told me so many stories about this place, but I never had a good reason to visit."

"Oh? Now, that makes me curious; what kind of stories?" Julie asked.

"Well, he was just turning thirteen when your great-grandfather passed away. He used to do odd jobs around town in the summers to make a bit of spending money, and he always said the oddest was the one he did for Ed Hayward."

"What was that?"

"Edward paid him to dig holes around the property."

"Really?" Julie asked. "Did he ever say what they were looking for?"

"Not as far as I know, but Brody said he thought your grandfather seemed a bit desperate about the whole thing. Edward had a map of the property with a grid drawn on it. In every square of the grid, they dug several holes of varying depths and then filled them back in." Tamara explained.

"Did they dig up the entire property?"

"I don't think so. My brother still has a copy of that map with the grids marked; would you like to see it?"

"Yes, I would. Now, how about a tour of the place and then we can get down to work," Julie replied.

Julie quickly showed Tamara through the house, and then, together, they unpacked the small tote full of jewelry. A few test shots showed the neutral gray backdrop worked well to showcase the colors and textures of the beads and gemstones. Working as a team, Tamara arranged the pieces while Julie took reflective light meter readings and made the necessary adjustments to her camera settings. The two quickly fell into a rhythm and two hours saw the entire project finished.

"Let me know if you ever decide to change careers and become a photographer's assistant. That was a great shoot." Julie stretched her back to get rid of a few kinks. After transferring the images to her laptop, she and Tamara scrolled through the entire series. Deciding they looked good and none of them needed re-shooting, Julie copied them onto a flash drive while Tamara repacked the jewelry.

After settling on a time frame for retouching the images, Tamara said she would have the map ready when Julie came by to drop them off in a few days. As Julie watched Tamara drive away, she wondered what she had gotten herself into; the thought of buried treasure on the property that in all these years had never been found just seemed ludicrous. If Edward and Brody had dug up large sections of the acreage, they should have found something. Maybe the map would provide more information about what or where the magic garden might be, but Julie doubted it would.

Deciding to take a break entirely from the idea of treasure hunting for the rest of the night, Julie ordered in her favorite pepperoni and black olive pizza, poured herself a generous glass of red wine, and popped a chick flick into the DVD player. When the movie was over, she settled into bed with a good book before falling asleep.

Sometime during the night, Julie jerked awake. She thought she had heard the murmuring of voices; but now, with the beat of her pounding heart echoing in her ears, she couldn't tell if the sounds had been part of a dream or real. Forcing herself to take deep, calming breaths she was finally able to quiet her blood enough to really listen. Old houses often made odd creaking noises. Sometimes it was the plumbing. Sometimes the noises were caused by the house settling. Julie was used to those types of noises, but this was different. It was not her imagination; she definitely heard voices coming from the library down the hall.

It took all of Julie's courage to get out of bed, grab her cell phone--in case she needed to call 911--and the fire poker for self-defense before creeping carefully, silently down the carpeted hall. After living here for more than half her life, she knew exactly which creaky floorboards to avoid. As she neared the library door, she could see it was ajar, and there was a faint bluish light flickering somewhere in the interior.

Kneeling down to prevent whoever had broken into the house from seeing her so easily, Julie peered around the corner before letting out a choked cry.

Seated in two of the leather chairs were her dead grandmother and the man she recognized from the painting in the hall, her also dead, great-grandfather.

The painting had not done him justice. Even sitting down, she could tell he had been a tall man with rosy, freckled skin. Soft hair faded to the yellow-tinted white that marked him as having been a natural redhead was combed back to frame a kindly face.

Both appeared as solid as Julie herself but with a faint bluish light hovering around their bodies. Her quiet cry drew their attention to her as she knelt in the doorway, too shocked to move into the room.

"Come in, dear girl," her grandmother said; but Julie was rooted to the floor, mouth agape.

"Yes, girl; get in here and have a seat. There is much to discuss, even if there is little we can tell you," her great-grandfather Julius said, gesturing with what appeared to be a lit pipe. Though he spoke impatiently, she could tell his gruffness was not aimed at her, but at whatever outside force kept him from speaking plainly.

Shaking her head in disbelief, Julie got to her feet and slowly walked into the room.

Chapter Six

"Is this real?" Julie asked as she slowly sank to the floor to sit cross-legged on the patterned rug. She was tempted to reach out a hand and see if Grams was as solid as she appeared, but couldn't quite bring herself to find out.

"Reality is overrated," her grandmother replied dryly but with a twinkle in her eye. "Now listen up; we don't have much time. We can't tell you anything directly, but we can give you a few hints to help you on your way."

"First things first," her great-grandfather interrupted, "You need to watch out for treachery, treachery, and betrayal. It's in those blasted papers; be careful about those papers."

"Which papers? The map of where Edward was digging, something from the historian?"

"Can't say more. Just remember what I said; pay attention to those papers," agitation evident in his expression he waved his pipe in the air for emphasis. Again, Julie understood his impatience had nothing to do with her, but at his inability to communicate effectively.

"Okay, I'll try to remember," she answered as the bluish halo began to slowly flicker and fade from around her great-grandfather.

She turned to her grandmother, still shocked and unsure whether she was awake or dreaming. "Are you ghosts?" she asked. "I always told Gustavia she was crazy for believing in auras and spirits, but maybe I was the crazy one after all."

"Nothing ever dies; especially when there is love. And I do love you, my child," Grams answered. "Now, listen closely. We don't have much time before it will be too late for this cycle."

"First, remember what your great-grandfather said, be careful of those papers." Julie nodded impatiently and gestured for Grams to continue.

"Second, remember this: the magic garden will bring the light; don't think so literally." With that statement there was a flash of light, then both chairs were empty. On the table between them lay the family history she had spent hours searching for in that very room.

After a moment, she hesitantly reached out to touch the spot where Grams had been sitting. She felt a quick, mild tingle, then nothing: no warmth, no evidence to show what she had seen was real.

Getting to her feet – and deciding her legs, though slightly shaky, would hold her – she snatched up the book, made her way down the hall, and then slid into bed. Julie was sure there was absolutely no way she would ever get back to sleep; yet, in what seemed like only a few short minutes, she opened her eyes and realized it was morning.

Her memories from the night before were fresh and detailed, but with a surreal quality that allowed Julie to almost convince herself it had all been an extremely vivid dream. Even so, her first action after getting out of bed was to rush to the library and look for evidence to support her middle-of-the-night experience. At first, she saw nothing—no telltale indentations in the seats, no marks where feet might have rested and flattened the fibers of the carpet. Nothing appeared out of place until, just as she was getting ready to leave, she noticed a tiny bit of pipe ash on the arm of the chair where her great-grandfather had been sitting. Remembering the book she had carried back to her room, Julie walked slowly down the hall to check. It was there, right on her nightstand where she'd dropped it on her way back to bed.

A dream? No, it was real. Everything she had seen and heard the night before was real. Maybe she should start braiding her hair and wearing little strings of bells around her neck.

Later that morning, Julie placed a call to the historian who had compiled her family history. Barrett Kingsley, it turned out, was in poor health and his memory was fading; but he still had his collection of notes and would have his grandson Tyler drop them off for Julie to read. He couldn't recall any mention of a magic garden; but assured her, if there were any information, it would be in his notes.

Then, back in her studio, Julie began resetting the lighting for her next series of images. The concept for the series had come to her in a store dressing room. There had been mirrors attached to a set of folding doors and the play of images as they opened and closed had inspired her to play with reflections. She laid large pieces of square, round, and rectangular mirrored glass on the floor; propped more pieces of mirror against boxes, tripods, and furniture; then arranged various objects around and on the mirrors creating a sort of kaleidoscope effect. Lighting was a bit tricky since the mirrors refracted the light in unpredictable ways. She experimented with a soft-box fitted with a warming filter and then with some tightly directed spotlights. After a few test shots, she added some colored filters to the spotlights then shot some more.

After an hour or so of repositioning, relighting, and re-shooting, she was close to having something workable. Experimenting with various angles and distances, she decided she was well on her way to creating a series of compelling abstract images; powerful, but subtle and mysterious. Sort of like the turn her life was taking.

Looking at her watch, she realized she was running behind schedule. Logan would be picking her up any minute now for their trip to the lawyer's office to go over the documents he'd had drawn up. She was annoyed at the pressure Logan had been putting on her about these matters. Her irritation was compounded by having asked several times for copies of the prenuptial agreement and the wills so she could read them over, only to be told they were just standard boilerplate documents. Logan said he didn't want her to have to worry about what he called "minor" details, but she was still uneasy and more than a bit annoyed.

Everything that had happened over the past few days was making her feel edgy. Maybe that was why she felt so unsettled in her relationship; she wondered if it might have been better to cancel the appointment altogether, but it was too late for that.

He arrived exactly on time—Logan was a stickler for punctuality—gave her a quick peck on the cheek and fairly pulled her out the door. All the way to the lawyer's office he chatted away about his work, cutting Julie off with yet another story each time she tried to speak. She wanted to tell him about the magic garden, but he never gave her a chance.

When he finally pulled the car into the parking lot of the tidy office building where his lawyer practiced, she had subsided into silence. Logan was thankful she had stopped protesting; this was the first step in his carefully laid plan, and she was not going to mess it up.

"Julie, this is my lawyer, Justin Abernathy. Justin, meet my fiancée, Julie Hayward."

"It's nice to meet you," she said.

"The pleasure is mine," he replied.

"Can we get started?" Logan hurriedly cut in, putting a stop to any further pleasantries.

"Yes, sure," Justin turned his attention back to Julie. "I assume Logan gave you copies of the documents so you could read them over and have your own attorney make any necessary changes."

"No, I actually haven't seen any copies; Logan assured me this paperwork was all standard, and I didn't need to retain my own attorney," she looked at Logan and saw his face was flushed with barely contained annoyance.

"Julie," he said, "if you trust me at all, you'll just sign the papers." He pushed, trading on her feelings to guilt her into signing.

"It isn't that I don't trust you, Logan. But even your own attorney thinks I should have the chance to read them first."

For a split second, Julie thought she saw a look of hatred flash across Logan's face before he composed his features into an expression of concern. Now she was angry and did not bother to try and hide it. Normally Julie considered herself an even-tempered person, but after the last few days, her emotions seemed just a bit too close to the surface and were not as easily controlled. She turned her furious gaze on him: eyes blazing, foot tapping out a staccato beat; she did not speak.

"I was just trying to take care of you; you know that, right?" His voice turned wheedling. At this point, Logan realized he might have been a bit too forceful. He had never seen Julie get angry; she was usually so tractable that, in his head, he had nicknamed her the country mouse. Now, he was beginning to think he'd made a mistake with her; she might not be as easy to handle as he expected. That was bad. He'd been positive she would fall in line without questioning his motives.

"Yes, but I am an adult; I can take care of myself." To Justin, she said, "Thank you; I will take a copy of those documents. Once I've had a chance to read them, we will get back to you. I am sorry to have taken so much of your time."

"It's not a problem; just call for an appointment whenever you're ready.

You can have your attorney contact me with any questions," he said pointedly. And with that, Julie took the proffered envelope and sailed out the door. She was tempted to tell Logan to just leave without her, but she wasn't up to the walk back to the house.

Thankfully, considering the chill pervading the atmosphere inside the car, the drive home was short. Logan appeared calm, but Julie could sense that, under his polite exterior, he was seething, angry. She wasn't exactly impressed with him, either. Knowing it was better to have everything out in the open, Julie described her visit to the psychic – glossing over the more unbelievable aspects of her recent experiences–– and explained that there might be something of value hidden in or around the old house. She did not mention anything about her middle-of-the-night ghostly visit but told him what little she remembered of the deathbed tale. Julie then waited to see his response.

Exactly as expected, he was completely dismissive.

"Don't be silly; that sounds more farfetched than one of Hattie McBatty's children's stories."

"Calling my best friend names is not helping, Logan."

The rest of the trip was silent. By the time they pulled up in front of the house, Logan had calmed himself and said, "Please, just read through the papers; can't you see I'm only trying to show you how much I love you by protecting your interests." He smiled as though nothing had happened, then gave Julie a quick peck of a kiss, and, not seeming to notice her lack of response, drove away. Julie stood on the steps watching his car disappear down the drive. How had she never noticed this side of him? Smarmy one minute and overbearing the next, he ignored anything that conflicted with his own idea of what was correct.

He also didn't notice the shimmer that arrowed from the formal garden into his back seat. Called by Julie's distress—and with the perspective lent by being a ghost—Grams knew her beloved granddaughter was upset about something, and she was going to do her part to save the day. She just needed to figure out how.

Clutching the manila envelope, Julie stalked up the steps and let herself into the house muttering imprecations under her breath. Until recently, her relationship with Logan had seemed like a mature meeting of the minds between two adults. Maybe he didn't think she had a temper since there had never been any reason for fighting, but if he continued the childish act he had put on today things were going to change.

Tossing the envelope onto the table, Julie began pacing from room to room, tension mounting into anger. What on earth had possessed Logan to think she would just merrily sign legal papers without even reading them first? Didn't he know her at all? He had watched her take care of Grams during her final weeks, had seen the care she had taken with the paperwork from each doctor. He and Gustavia had been beside her while she dealt with the funeral arrangements.

Julie frowned.

Wait, that wasn't quite true. Gustavia, tears streaming down her face, had helped choose an urn to hold Gram's ashes, had looked at the book of Thank You cards to find one with just the right artistic flair. Logan had taken a business call and gone outside for privacy. More than that, she remembered the same thing had happened on the day Grams died. While she and Gustavia watched Estelle slip away, Logan had been absorbed with work on his laptop because he'd had an "unavoidable" problem that had to be dealt with right then. Before Grams had been wheeled out of the house on her way to the funeral home, he said he needed to get back to the city. Oh, he made sure that Gustavia would be staying and had seemed concerned that Julie should not be alone; but, even so, he had gone. He had left her at a time when he should have been practically glued to her side.

Maybe Gustavia and Grams had been right about him all along. Neither one of them had ever warmed up to Logan, and the two of them had formed their own little non-admiration society for him. Julie told herself it was because they were both a bit overly protective, and they were both passionate women who expected relationships to be based on emotions. Julie had always prided herself on being more practical, more logical. Both had pronounced Logan to be a cold fish, and Gustavia maintained his aura was "hideously oozy," and he gave off bad vibes. Bad vibes, whatever those were, had not been enough to deter the relationship; and, when Logan proposed, Julie hadn't seen any good reason to say no. Marrying him seemed like the logical thing to do. After all, she was not like Gustavia, not like Grams, not like her own mother who put passion before safety.

So Logan didn't inspire her to the heights of ardent infatuation, so what? Passion was overrated and almost always got a person into trouble.

Oh, my God, she thought, **maybe I'm the cold fish**. But when anger flashed through her again – turning her face hot, clenching her fists, and causing everything inside of her to rise up and churn – she decided she was not cold or emotionless; not at all.

When Julie was angry, her first impulse was to dive into housework. Cleaning let her burn off steam while getting something positive done. She was angry enough right now to clean the entire house and then move on to the neighbors.

She barely had time to change into a comfortable pair of leggings and an old t-shirt before she heard the doorbell ringing. Expecting a contrite Logan to be on the other side of the door, and

not at all ready to make up, she twisted
the knob and yanked it open.

Chapter Seven

Well, that's not Logan, she thought as she hesitantly said, "Hello, may I help you?"

"Are you Julie? I'm Tyler Kingsley; my grandfather asked me to drop these notes off for you."

"Yes, thank you; I hope it wasn't too much trouble," she answered. "I wasn't expecting you to come so quickly."

"No, no trouble at all, my schedule was wide open for the day." He smiled a bit sheepishly, deep blue eyes twinkling. "Besides, I'm willing to admit I do have an ulterior motive; if you don't mind, I would love to see the house. I've read the history and the notes my grandfather made, and I've always wanted to see it for myself."

"Sure, least I can do." Julie, still trying to tame her emotions, took a deep breath and let it out on a sigh. His timing was not stellar, but she might as well be polite.

Tyler ran a hand through dark, glossy hair just long enough to curl over his ears. She was upset about something. It wasn't hard to tell. He had sisters; he knew the signs. He let his eyes rove over her gently, assessing her body language: tense across the shoulders, chin slightly raised, and her eyes were still snapping even though he could see she was trying to tamp it down. Something had gotten under her skin.

Now he was doubly curious; and the best way to satisfy curiosity, in his experience, was to investigate. So, knowing full well she was in no mood to be cordial, he followed her into the house anyway.

She led him, first to the kitchen, where she offered him a cold drink. After pouring them both a glass of lemonade, she asked if he wanted to see just the house or some of the property as well. He wanted to see it all, so she decided to start outside with the formal garden.

As they strolled through the smooth green expanse of the back lawn, Julie told him the garden now occupied only about three-quarters of its former size. For the past few years, the local garden club had maintained this two-acre section of the property in exchange for being able to bring tour groups through on Sunday afternoons. It was a nice source of revenue for the group and saved Julie a ton of time and money; making it a win-win situation.

"Do you think this is the **magic garden**?" Tyler looked around him avidly. Julie tilted her head and looked at him. So, there had been something in the notes about the magic garden, though she'd seen nothing in her scan of the resulting book. Clearly, Barrett Kingsley had forgotten after all this time. She wasn't sure how she felt about Tyler knowing her family secrets. He had been watching her slowly relax as they walked across the property, but now the tension was back; she just kept feeding his curiosity.

"I doubt it; Grams and her garden club renovated it when I was in high school. In the process, they dug up pretty much every square inch of this section. If there had been anything to find, I am sure they would have found it."

"What if one of the garden club members found something and kept quiet?"

Surprised at her own reaction, Julie turned and said hotly, "Those garden club members were my grandmother's closest friends. They would never steal from her; not for anything."

Tyler held up both hands in surrender, "Sorry; it was just a thought; I didn't mean anything by it. Sometimes I don't use the filter that should be between my brain and my mouth."

Not completely mollified but willing to give him the benefit of the doubt, Julie led him past the formal garden and up a slight incline. At the top of the knoll, she stopped and gestured for him to look around. This slightly heightened vantage point overlooked most of the property's acreage.

A series of smaller perennial beds edged a wide expanse of mowed lawn leading down to the line of trees marking the boundary of the planted areas. Julie explained there was additional acreage beyond the trees that had been cleared for vegetable gardening at one time.

"I was thinking of dividing some of the cleared areas into smaller parcels and selling them to pay for repairs to the house. Then this business with . . . well, something came up, and right now that is not an option."

Tyler looked at Julie, eyes narrowed speculatively. He had picked up on the hesitation. "Business with what?"

Julie blushed and replied, "Trust me, you don't want to know."

He quirked an eyebrow, "Sure I do, what happened? Did you find a treasure map? I read all the notes, and there was no mention of a map."

"Not exactly; and you wouldn't believe me if I told you, so just let it go." The funny thing was – even funnier since she had no such compulsion to share her late-night visitation with Logan – Julie found herself tempted to tell him exactly what happened: all of it, including the most recent ghostly encounter. Logan already thought Gustavia belonged in the loony bin; she didn't want him to think of her that way as well. But she had a feeling Tyler wouldn't judge. It would be a relief to just get it out of her system.

Now Tyler was even more intrigued; there was a story here, and he had a firm rule never to let the opportunity to hear a good story pass without digging into it.

"C'mon, give. How do you know I wouldn't believe you if you don't at least tell me what happened?"

This guy was worse than a dog with a bone, but Julie had the sense his interest was genuine. Surprisingly, her gut told her she might even be able to trust him, but she needed to get to know him a little better first.

"Maybe another time."

Tyler let it go, reluctantly. His journalistic instinct told him the story was worth hearing, but he could see she was embarrassed by something. He made up his mind then and there to find out what. They began to walk back toward the formal garden.

"Anyway," she continued, "the only map I know of is a treasure-less one. My grandfather hired a local teenager to help him dig up a bunch of the property back in the day. They never found anything. The teenager turned out to be the brother of a friend of mine. He kept the map they used, and she's going to get me a copy."

Julie felt more than a bit uncomfortable even talking about the idea of looking for treasure. She wanted to embrace the project, be more like Gustavia who was always ready for a new experience; but something, some sense of impending vulnerability, held her back from making a total commitment to the idea of an adventure.

Her parents had gone on an adventure, and they never returned. Their last video shoot was in a rain forest. Understanding the dangers and having a premonition they chose, for the first time, to send their seven-year-old daughter – under protest – to stay with her grandparents. Partway through filming, the two left the compound to scout a new location and never returned. Two days later, searchers found their bodies at the bottom of a ravine. Julie was heartbroken.

The devastating loss turned her into an overly-cautious, highly-pragmatic child. Before losing her parents, she had been a bubbly, imaginative girl who loved starting out on any new adventure; now, the only place she let that fanciful sideshow was through her work. Photography was the only area in her life she approached without reserve.

"So, what is it that makes a garden **magic**? I mean, this garden looks magical; but if there's nothing here, you might be missing some other logical criteria, "Tyler turned in a circle, gesturing at the gardens, "What other options have you explored?" he asked. Reading his grandfather's notes the night before, he had quickly clued in on the one section that seemed most likely to have sparked her sudden interest in the notes.

Then his mouth dropped open.

"Whoa, who is that?" Tyler, with eyebrows raised, gazed past Julie with a dazed expression. Turning, she saw Gustavia in full regalia making her way across the lawn. Today she was decked out in a batik skirt in shades of turquoise and yellow, paired with a salmon-colored tank top, and enough jewelry to weigh down the Titanic. Tied over the skirt were at least two of the jingly hip scarves worn by belly dancers. Woven into her braids, Julie could see several keys and what appeared to be several small Christmas ornaments. Where Logan would have been rolling his eyes in disgust, Tyler, with a huge grin plastered across his face, strode forward holding out a hand in greeting.

"This is my friend Gustavia," Julie introduced the two. "And Gustavia, please meet Tyler Kingsley; his grandfather was the historian who researched our family. Tyler was kind enough to drop off his grandfather's notes."

"With rings on her fingers and bells on her toes, And she shall have music wherever she goes," he said, quoting Mother Goose. Then, bowing low before Gustavia, he kissed her hand. To Julie, he said, "I didn't know you were friends with a goddess. This day just gets better and better."

Turning to Julie, Gustavia said, "He really needs to meet Kat and Amethyst!"

"More goddesses? Yes; please, bring them on! I can't wait."

"Amethyst is an aura reader, and Kat is a psychic medium," Gustavia explained gravely.

"To tell you the truth, my queen, when I met Julie here, I got the feeling she was a bit repressed; you know, a little uptight. She must have hidden depths to have friends like you."

"Well, she has her moments, but we do the best we can to keep her from crawling into her shell." Gustavia grinned in delight.

"Excuse me--I'm standing right here," Julie rolled her eyes.

"Did she tell you about the..." Gustavia began before Julie cut her off.

"That's enough; Tyler is not interested in my personal business; I only just met him half an hour ago. Maybe we could wait a day or so before we air all of my dirty laundry."

"Oooh, dirty laundry is it," he interjected, "I am intrigued." And to his surprise, he found he was. Even if he had been correct in his first assumption that she was a bit tightly wound, Julie was certainly attractive; and, with friends like Gustavia, there must be some whimsy under all that outward stiffness. Plainly, there were a few layers to explore. Besides, what red-blooded male could resist a treasure hunt?

Chapter Eight

Gustavia reached down into her voluminous straw bag and pulled out two pieces of heavy wire. The pieces were about 2 feet long with a 90-degree bend some 6 inches in on one end. Grabbing the pieces by the smaller section and holding them level in front of her at shoulder width apart, Gustavia walked slowly toward the garden.

Tyler looked at Julie and tilted his head toward Gustavia. She shrugged in response and waived a hand indicating he should just go ahead and ask the question himself.

"What are you doing?"

"Dowsing. My friend Luka Proud taught me how to do it."

"Interesting."

"He says you have to have a bit of intuition and a powerful connection to the earth; it's mostly used to find water, but some people resonate with metals so I figured it might work for finding treasure, too."

"A perfectly reasonable assumption."
He watched with fascination as
Gustavia marched through the garden.
He thought about suggesting a metal
detector but decided dowsing was more
fun to watch.

"Hey, Jules, where do you think I
should check? Any ideas where the
magic garden might be?" Gustavia
called back over her shoulder.

"Well, since the garden club dug up
most of this area, I think you'd better
try somewhere else." She explained
about Tamara's brother and his map.
"Maybe if you wait a few days, you can
use the map and just concentrate on

the areas that haven't already been covered."

"In the meantime," Tyler said, "to test your dowsing prowess, I'll hide some treasure for you to find." Julie shook her head. It usually didn't pay to encourage one of Gustavia's schemes but, clearly, this situation had gone out of her control.

Excited as a kitten with a new ball of yarn, Gustavia dodged behind the nearest tree and began counting down from a hundred while Tyler emptied the loose change and keys from his pockets into a crevice between two rocks bordering the garden. Julie, mentally throwing up her hands in surrender, stalked over to a wrought iron garden bench and made herself comfortable. After watching the spectacle for a few moments, she arose and headed back to the house to retrieve her camera. Gustavia, arms outstretched in her unconventional clothing did look a bit like a goddess—well, maybe a wonky goddess—but it was definitely a Kodak moment.

Now it was Tyler's turn to sit on the bench and watch the spectacle. As Gustavia moved around the garden, Julie alternately climbed on rocks or crouched near the ground to shoot from varying perspectives. Before long, Gustavia neared the area where he'd secured the cache of coins. Up until now, the metal rods had not budged; but, as she walked within a couple yards of the coins, the rods twitched, and her eyes widened. "Whoa, check this out," Gustavia said. "It's working."

"Holy crap," Tyler said, "it is."

With each step closer to the hidden coins, the rods swung more quickly until, finally, they snapped together and pointed right at the spot. Gustavia reached between the rocks, grabbed the coins and began to dance. Tyler joined her, hopping up and down in excitement while Julie continued shooting: though now, it was his face she was tightly focused on, capturing the excitement glinting in those deep blue eyes.

"I did it, I did it, I did it," Gustavia sang out.

She and her dowsing rods were about to become a fixture on the property. **No doubt about it,** Julie thought resisting the urge to roll her eyes.

"I cannot tell you how happy I am," Julie said dryly. One thing though, having something else to do might keep Gustavia from dragging her off to see more psychics and aura readers. Silver linings. Every cloud has them.

Gustavia looked toward the house.

"Uh-oh, here comes the wet blanket," she said. She and Logan were always coldly civil to each other; but, for her friend's sake, she wiped the disdain from her face and greeted him cordially as he joined them on the lawn.

Logan had barely gotten halfway back to the city before hearing what he thought was his own mental voice telling him Julie must have read those papers by now and, maybe, he should go back. Unseen in the back seat, Grams smiled, delighted at her ability to make her whisper heard as Logan made an illegal U-turn.

Positive he would find his fiancé contritely waiting for him, he'd sped back to the house.

Julie introduced the two men. Barely acknowledging Tyler, Logan took Julie by the arm stating, "We need to talk," as he pulled her forcefully away.

Tyler and Gustavia exchanged a look. He was not impressed. This guy had gone from zero to jackass in under 30 seconds.

"Not now, Logan, I have guests." She tried to pull her arm away, but he only tightened his grip.

"This is important; have you looked at those papers yet?" he asked, ignoring everything but his own interests. Still holding her arm, he leaned closer to Julie. Too close. He loomed over her. Tyler took a deep breath, ready to defend this woman he had only just met when Julie, eyes alight with anger, shook off Logan's hand and took a step forward. "Don't try to intimidate me, Logan." She drilled a finger into his chest. "I don't want to hear another word about those papers today, and you are unforgivably rude."

Logan's eyes widened in surprise; he hadn't expected resistance. He'd used what he considered to be a perfect set of skills on her; she should have been trained by now to fall in line with whatever he asked. He clenched his hand into a fist, the desire to use it nearly overwhelming.

"I will read them when I get the chance," she continued.

Without another word, he turned and stalked away across the lawn.

Face flaming red, Logan got into his car. He needed to calm down before he messed up the entire plan. Venting his frustration by slamming the car into gear, he was tempted to peel out but drove sedately away. It wouldn't be a good idea to let anyone see the rage building up inside him. When he let the beast out of its cage, people sometimes got hurt. Now was not the time.

What was her deal, anyway? He'd expected her to just meekly sign the papers. Instead of thinking he might possibly have been wrong in his personality assessment of Julie, he decided Gustavia was the one turning her against him with all this talk of hidden valuables. Well, that was something he could easily deal with. It shouldn't take much to break up that little friendship; they were nothing alike and had only known each other for a few years. They couldn't be that close; and if smashing their friendship didn't work, there was a more permanent solution. That crazy witch was not going to come between him and his future.

Six months of research on Hayward House hadn't turned up any rumors of treasure. Instead, Logan's master plan was to get control of the property then sell it to developers. In anticipation of everything going according to plan, he had already proposed a deal for the property to be developed into high-end condos, making him a lot of money in the process. The house would be razed; it was the land that had value. This was his big score. After all, it had only taken him three months to convince that half-witted twit to marry him; it shouldn't take long to get her to sign those papers; then he could do whatever he wanted with the house and the land. There would be no stopping him.

He knew when to step in and play the gallant prince. The grandmother had just loved him; then, when she died, he had swept Julie off her feet counting on her intense grief to be a big enough distraction that she would fall in line with his plans. Once he had the house--well, there was no way he was going to spend a lifetime with that boring little photographer, not when he had a hot calendar model as a side piece: gorgeous, yes; but also dumber than a bag of hammers. Just the way he liked them.

Learning there might be something of value in the house or on the property made him doubly intent on following through with his goal. He would become the sole owner of Hayward house at any cost, plunder everything it had to offer, then walk away.

Descended from a long line of pirate ancestors, he planned to carry on his heritage and its traditions—on land, of course; that was where the money was these days. He would stop at nothing— not even murder—to get what he wanted, what he already considered was his.

He still didn't see the shimmer in his rear seat; nor did he feel the intense fury coming from the energy of the spirit sitting there, the spirit that was easily able to read his thoughts. This man had no idea what forces he was messing with, but Grams was about to unleash a beast of her own. She'd gotten him to at least begin showing his true colors already hadn't she? It was a start.

"Well, that was pleasant," Tyler said, "nice to meet you, too." He and Gustavia shared a conspiratorial eye roll.

Julie slanted him a look, "I'm sorry you had to see that, but at least we got our first major fight out of the way before the **wedding**." Bothered more than he expected to be by the word wedding, Tyler said, "That was your first fight?" His eyebrows arched in surprise. "That was not a fight. That was an exercise in intimidation." His eyes narrowed as he replayed the scene in his head.

Gustavia muttered something under her breath. Tyler couldn't help being amused as he picked up the words **skunk** and **stripes**.

Julie looked away.

"But," he continued, "you handled it well. Can I be nosy and ask what papers?"

"A prenup, a will, and life insurance."

"Be careful signing those papers." As he said the words, she heard her grandfather's voice and felt a chill that raised the hairs on the back of her neck. Gustavia stepped closer, tilted her head and got that look on her face.

The one that said she was about to talk about auras or chakras or some other new age word ending in **ras**.

She didn't quite know how it happened, but fifteen minutes later all three of them were in the car headed toward Amethyst's house. Or was it a burrow? Julie wasn't sure what to call it; she also didn't know how Tyler had managed to get invited along. Turning to him she asked, "Don't you have anything better to do?"

"Better than meeting more of your fascinating friends? Nope." He crossed his arms and gave her a cheeky grin.

Julie slumped in her seat and then stared out the window. How had her life gotten this out of control in a matter of days?

Meanwhile, Gustavia gave Tyler the rundown on auras.

"Yours is wide, and Julie's is tall, but they are almost the same color pattern which is cool. I just wish I could see mine, but they don't show up in mirrors," she said as she drove north toward the hills outside of town, "Amethyst says my dominant colors are blue shading to indigo. In chakra colors that means my intuition and spirituality centers are strongest."

By now, Logan would have been talking over Gustavia to shut her up. No--strike that. Logan would never have gotten into a car with her in the first place, but Tyler asked questions as though he were genuinely interested. He listened to the answers. Now to see what he would make of Amethyst. This might be a little bit fun.

For the second time in less than a week, Julie trudged through the seemingly empty field leading to the cozy underground home. For the second time in less than a week, her aura was going to be observed, talked about and repaired. For the second time in less than a week, she wished she were anywhere but here.

Chapter Nine

A gorgeous photographer who lived in what could almost pass for a castle, a treasure hunt, a goddess, and now he was pretty sure he was about to meet a fairy. A fairy that lived under a hill. Grabbing Julie's hand, Tyler placed it on his arm and said, "Pinch me; go ahead; do it."

They each felt a little tingle in the spot where her hand rested on his arm, but they both had their own compelling reasons for ignoring the feeling.

Shaking her head, she snatched her hand back, but grinned at him and said, "You haven't seen the half of it."

Tyler felt a great sense of anticipation as he looked at the door set into the hill. Made from honey-colored wood, it was attached with black wrought-iron hinges and covered with carvings in the shape of climbing vines. Flowers in shades of pink and white burst out of window boxes cleverly constructed from pieces of old rain gutter. When the door opened, and he laid eyes on Amethyst for the first time, Tyler grinned like a dolphin. Best day ever. He didn't even wait for anyone to introduce him, just walked right up and kissed her on both cheeks saying, "I'm Tyler, and you must be the queen of the fairies."

His unabashed glee couldn't help but communicate itself to Amethyst, and she let out the throaty laugh that never failed to surprise. "What have you brought me, Gustavia?" she asked. Playing along, Gustavia answered, "Oh, just a mere mortal; feed him, and legend says he will be trapped here forever."

Before Amethyst could answer, Tyler pulled something out of his pocket.

"This here is a musket ball I always carry with me; I believe cold iron will protect me from the fairy's spell."

The three dissolved into laughter as Julie shook her head and grinned. Crazy they were, every single one of them; but it warmed her heart to see Gustavia take to someone so quickly. Even though she was the most generous, caring person Julie had ever met, people were often put off by her outward appearance and what was considered, at best, a quirky personality. Watching her bond with Tyler throughout this strange afternoon had been a joyful experience. Since she was about to get outed for seeing ghosts, she supposed she should take her enjoyment wherever she could find it.

Finally, Amethyst turned to Julie and said, "Well, what in the world have you done to yourself now? Your aura is totally wonky."

First rumpled, now wonky. Her aura was taking a beating this week. Face red as a fire engine, Julie looked away and mumbled, "I saw a ghost."

That did it; now all their attention was focused on her. She looked into three pairs of widened eyes and repeated more loudly, "I saw a ghost, okay. Well, two of them actually; Grams and great-grandfather, last night in the library. They talked to me, and I know it was real because he was smoking a pipe and the ashes were on the chair this morning. I wasn't hallucinating, and I'm not crazy." Her voice rose in self-defense, though it needn't have because all three nodded at her as if this were the most ordinary news in the world.

"Well, of course, you did. Kat opened the door, and it's obvious you have some latent psychic abilities," Gustavia nodded as she spoke not noticing this pronouncement nearly blew the top of Julie's head off.

"I am not psychic," Julie spoke through gritted teeth. "Nothing like this has ever happened to me before; and, in fact, I blame you Gustavia for taking me to see that Kat woman in the first place." Tears burned in her eyes as the frustration of the past few days overwhelmed her again. Immediately Gustavia went to her and enveloped Julie in a comforting hug.

"It's been a bit much for her to take in all at once," she said, glancing up at Tyler to see his reaction. Satisfied by the look of empathy on his face, she once again installed her friend on the cushioned area and went to make tea while Amethyst began a guided meditation.

Tyler watched the entire spectacle with interest. This was a new world with the most incredible inhabitants.

This time Julie actually paid attention as Amethyst directed her to imagine herself walking through a sunny meadow. Inch by inch she relaxed into the suggested rhythmical breathing pattern until, with a sigh, she fully surrendered. In that split second, all the tension left her body, and she heard Gustavia say, "That's done it."

Seeing absolutely no difference other than Julie being truly relaxed for the first time that day, Tyler accepted that her wonky aura had been healed and now it was time for tea. Today's special was a nice cinnamon flavor with a touch of agave nectar. It tasted like the Atomic Fireball candies he had loved as a child.

There was little he could contribute to the conversation, but he was captivated by the idea of seeing an aura. Finally, he asked if there were a trick to it and if anyone could see them. Amethyst asked Julie to sit in a chair in front of a blank area of the wall then had Tyler sit directly across from her.

Amethyst explained how he needed to relax his eyes and his focus. Then she told him not to look at Julie but to look at the wall around her using his peripheral vision. He should expect to see the aura hovering a couple of inches away from the wall. "Think of it like those 3D image things so popular in the '90s; it works about the same way," she said. "And once you start seeing them, sometimes it becomes hard to stop."

"How will I know if I see it?" he asked.

"It will look a bit like a rainbow."

It might have been easier to see the aura if he weren't distracted by looking at Julie herself. She sat in the chair, clearly caught between embracing the concept of aura-viewing and being embarrassed by the very idea, humor at herself and also at the situation evident in the sparkle of her eyes and the quirk of her lips. Tyler could tell she would rather not believe in something that might be considered nonsense, but she was beginning to take it seriously in spite of herself. He doubted she would start wearing bells in her hair and gossamer clothing; but in her own quiet way, once committed to the reality, she would never waver.

He liked that about her. He liked that, in the space of one bizarre afternoon, he was starting to get to know her. She was reserved in some ways, yet still open, and it was clear she cared about her friends enough to step into their world even when it made her uncomfortable. That told him she had an adventurous side.

Too bad she was engaged. Though, if that scene today was any indication, she might not stay that way. It hadn't taken him long to see there were big problems with that relationship. The biggest one being she was engaged to a weasel, but it looked like she was beginning to catch on. When she did, he figured she would do the right thing. One could only hope.

Since conversation on the ride back centered mainly on auras, Julie stayed quiet. She was feeling better; less chaotic in her thoughts, but still anxious. If those papers Logan was so insistent she sign contained betrayal and treachery as Grams and Julius had said, then she needed to see them right away. There had not been time to grab them before the wonky aura trip. She also needed to make an appointment of her own with an attorney, one she could trust. Then, depending on what she found, there would be some decisions to make.

It hurt to think she might have made a mistake with Logan, but she was starting to think she had, and a big one. She had been so sure in the beginning, but lately, he'd been acting churlish and had belittled her at every opportunity. It was humiliating to think her decision to enter a relationship based on logic might be faulty: that romantic feelings might be vitally important and that Logan did not respect her in the way she'd thought. Looking back on their relationship, Julie began to see how often she'd turned a blind eye to any number of warning signs that things were not going well. Maybe passion shouldn't be the sole basis for a relationship, but it was becoming obvious that the lack of it wasn't healthy either.

Clearly, something was wrong and had been for some time, but she wasn't quite sure where it had gone off the rails. At what point had Logan begun to think his recent treatment of her was justified? Now, it was time to take a good, long look at how things had evolved. She'd known Logan for several months; they'd only been engaged for a few weeks. Was that really enough time to be sure? Was he the right man? Was this the love of a lifetime?

Grams had not raised Julie to be a fool. Instead, she had instilled in her granddaughter healthy self-esteem and a rather large dose of common sense. It wasn't that Julie totally discounted romantic love; she knew the best relationships had some spark, some sizzle, as long as it was balanced with respect and admiration. Physical attraction shouldn't be the only priority, but now she could see that she had been so focused on avoiding a relationship based solely on romance that she had chosen one completely devoid of it. She also realized that she was missing another element in her life: today, even with all the ups and downs, had shown her she needed to have more fun.

Spending time watching Gustavia, Amethyst, and Tyler spar with each other had been entertaining; she hadn't realized how heavy her emotions had become until the laughter had lightened things up. It seemed it was time for a change. Grams would not want her to be sad and serious forever, and Julie wanted more out of lif

Chapter Ten

"Did you see that?" Estelle, better known as Grams, asked Julius. "I gave him a nudge, and his carefully constructed facade slipped enough for Julie to start to see through to the evil under the surface. Since she noticed, maybe now the blinders are off, and she will come to her senses.

"The two ghosts perched on the roof of the gazebo in the formal garden. From their vantage point, they could see the house, the driveway and a large portion of the rest of the property. Even if they couldn't physically do much to protect the house, they both felt it was worth keeping an eye out for anything nefarious. Neither of them had a good feeling about Logan.

"Did you hear his thoughts?" Julius asked. "He was broadcasting pretty clearly. He means to harm our girl. We have to stop him and fast. She isn't the only one he'll hurt if he gets the chance. That nice gypsy child is also in danger."

Estelle snorted, "Gustavia's no gypsy, but she has become part of the family; I love her as though she were my own granddaughter, and I won't have him hurt either one of them. We need to come up with a plan. After hearing his thoughts, I want him gone from here, gone from Julie's life. She deserves so much more," she continued.

Julius considered his daughter-in-law. They'd had a good relationship while he was alive, and he had genuinely liked the girl his son had married. Now, he liked her even more. She had spunk. He approved.

As the only son in a long line of only sons, Julius had continued the family tradition: passing Hayward house down to Edward, also an only son, who had forged a complicated relationship with his father. Julius was innovative, a free thinker, and flamboyant in his tastes while Edward was cautious, unimaginative, and unmotivated. Neither had much respect for the other and the only time Julius thought the boy had had any sense was when he married Estelle.

Edward had disapproved of his father's ongoing search for the next great invention. He thought Julius was wasting the money that should become his inheritance while Julius thought

Edward was spoiled rotten and didn't deserve the money that he hadn't done a thing to earn. A true man would make his own fortune; but Julius denied having wasted all of his money, though he was adamant if Edward could not handle his own finances, there was no reason for him to have control over what his father had earned. Having no other skills with which to make a living, and convinced his father was frittering away his entire inheritance, Edward decided it would be best if he joined the army and went to war. Injured during battle, he returned home but never fully regained his health.

Father and son continued their strained relationship until Julius became ill, but by then, it was too late to repair the rift. Edward followed his father only two short years later and did not live to see the birth of his son, Julie's father, Thomas.

Newly widowed, Estelle and her mother-in-law, Mary Lou, turned their home into a rooming house for other war-widowed women and their children. The women worked hard at converting a portion of the spacious grounds into vegetable gardens. They, with the help of their children, tilled the ground, planted and harvested the vegetables, fed themselves, then sold what was left over to pay expenses and keep their kids in clothes and shoes. Several years after Edward's death, Mary Lou suffered a burst appendix and died, which left the house to Estelle.

Eventually, all of the Weeping Widows, as they called themselves, had remarried and moved on, leaving Estelle alone in the big house with a young son and precious little income. Edward had been convinced there was a fortune still hidden somewhere on the grounds of Hayward House. He had often repeated the story of his father's dying declaration.

"He lay on the bed, barely breathing. Then he sat straight up—I don't know where he got the strength—then he said, 'use the key with the magic garden,' and I think he tried to point toward his left. 'It's all hidden; follow the light. Don't forget. Key--magic garden,' Then he was gone."

Estelle knew the story; knew it well, since she had been sitting there with her husband and mother-in-law at the foot of the bed. It was into her eyes Julius had been looking when he spoke his final words, but she also knew the story comforted her husband every time he told it. Still, she hadn't paid it much mind. If there had been anything of value to be found, surely Mary Lou must have known the hiding place and would have saved herself years of struggle with the proceeds from its contents.

Family records documented that quite a lot of heirloom silver and jewelry had been handed down through several generations. After Julius inherited, no one knew what had become of the items, and Estelle suspected they had been sold to fund another of her father-in-law's contraptions. It was possible he had hidden them somewhere, but she just didn't think so.

During the years following the loss of his father, Edward—so sure the magic garden was somewhere on the property—had dug holes all over the acreage in his zeal to find the family fortune. He never found a thing; but neither did he give up on the idea there was a treasure to be found, one that would take care of his family for a long time to come. Family legend said some of the silver pieces were of historical significance, as was at least one of the pieces of jewelry.

Estelle had not put much stock in the dying words of an eccentric man. Before her marriage, she'd worked for a short time at the hospital and knew the effect lack of oxygen had on the brain. This is what accounted for her father-in-law's rambling words. Whatever items of value he had once had, she was Julius had sold them and used the money on the odd inventions in the old workshop. None of them were worth anything. All of the money he had made, plus whatever had been handed down to him, was gone.

She struggled along for a few years, taking in boarders, keeping up some of the vegetable gardens, and selling the produce for extra money. Estelle was a talented painter and sculptor, but it was hard for a woman to sell artwork under her own name, so she used the pieces to decorate her home.

One bright, summer day a gentleman named James McLaren had come to her door asking to board for several weeks, and sparks flew:

between him and Estelle, yes, but also between him and her artwork. James was a traveling salesman—quite a successful one—but after falling in love with Estelle's paintings, he became her agent. Soon the two were married, and Estelle was making a comfortable living from her talent.

James was the perfect mate for Estelle: where she was expansive and flamboyant, he was understated and serious. He understood her creative needs, and she received commission after commission for large-scale paintings and sculpture. James became the only father young Tom had ever known, and the two got along famously. Tom inherited his mother's artistic bent and became a well-known, but underpaid, documentary filmmaker. He married Lisa, whom he met in film school; and, two years later, in the middle of shooting a documentary in South Africa, Julie was born.

Julius, unable to move on, had watched over Estelle, trying to communicate with her to let her know his last words had been true; but she never heard him, and he concluded the task of finding his hiding place was not for her. So he waited in frustration until she passed. Now she, like him, could not move on until this business was cleared up.

"I've been dead a good while longer than you; I've got a few tricks up my sleeve you aren't able to do yet. If he gets physical, I can take care of it, at least to a point."

"Okay. I can work around the edges of his mind, nudge him, get him to make a few more mistakes."

A shimmer of light is the most the naked eye would have picked up, even if looking directly at the gazebo roof. The only sound that carried across the still air was a faint whisper as Estelle and Julius made plans for dealing with Logan. Logan wouldn't know what hit him. He had picked the wrong mark this time, and he would pay for his mistake.

"And what about that nice blind psychic girl? What are we going to do about her? I feel pretty bad about using her the way we did, but desperate times and all."

"I think I can help her more. I already did help her a little. Did you notice you could see when you were speaking through her? Well, so could she. That means we might be able to do something to bring her vision back all the way," Estelle answered.

"Isn't that meddling? She told **the other girl** she chooses to be blind." Julius avoided saying Gustavia's name, finding it just too odd for his taste.

187

Even in death, he was a bit of an eccentric.

"Well, what we need to do is give her something she wants to see; I have some ideas on that front already. Nothing like a good man to open a woman's eyes."

Julius smirked, "That's not a very modern viewpoint."

"Modern has nothing to do with it; relationships are what make the world go around. Besides, if my hunch is right, we can kill two birds with one stone: by getting Gustavia to contact her brother about Logan, maybe she will reconnect with her family, and her brother will catch Logan. Someone has to stop Logan, or he will go on and do something like this again.

"So, what is our next move? Should we talk to Julie again, tell her...well, never mind, there isn't much we can tell her now, is there?"

"No," Estelle said, "she has to take the next step on her own. I have faith she will do the right thing; she is already starting to see that reprobate more clearly."

Julius ran a nearly transparent hand through his hair and sighed. "Do you think she'll find the first clue in time? I know she's smart, but she has to think creatively, or she's never going to find it."

"We have told her all we can; now it's time put the plan into action. Besides, that nice reporter boy was already beginning to get the right idea; he'll help her."

Streaks of light flew off the roof, headed in opposite directions. Estelle's first stop was to check in on Julie, then find a way to communicate with Gustavia. She felt bad about the necessity of this because she knew Gustavia's family had given her such a hard time. She had not been accepted or loved—quirks and all—but constantly pressured to change to fit in. This had been a painful situation. Estelle had no illusions that her actions might make things worse before they got better, but she still felt it was time for a reunion. Maybe even past time. She would do what she had to do.

Julius zipped into the city to keep tabs on Logan and see if he could learn what that scoundrel planned for his next move.

He quickly located the young man, pacing and ranting in his home office, doing a fine job of getting himself all worked up. It wasn't difficult to figure out he was beginning to realize Julie was not the pushover he had expected, and he was blaming Gustavia. From the sounds of Logan's thoughts, Julius became certain that the gypsy girl, as he preferred to think of her, was in danger. Estelle was right: the policeman brother needed to come help, and soon, or things could turn ugly.

Chapter Eleven

Tyler knew he should leave. Julie had already had a full day of it, but he still hadn't seen the house. If he never got another chance, he didn't want to miss this one. So, once Gustavia had left, he looked at Julie and said, "Think I could still get that tour?"

Julie raised one eyebrow, "You haven't had enough, yet?"

"Oh, no, not nearly," he grinned, attempting to appear harmless and hoping she would not kick him out. Tyler wanted to see it all: the museum, the library and the painting of Julius described in his grandfather's notes. Most of all, though, he wanted to talk Julie into letting him help look for the magic garden. If that meant spending more time with her, it would be no hardship. Besides, someone needed to keep an eye on that fiancé of hers; he was trouble. Some women liked their men a bit on the controlling side, but he didn't get that vibe from this one.

His mother had always teased him by saying he did great "Bambi eyes" when he wanted something. Figuring he had nothing to lose, he plaintively said, "Please," and turned them on Julie who laughed.

"Okay, no need to get all cute about it. Let's take the tour."

"Ah, she thinks I'm cute," he waggled his eyebrows and gave her an exaggerated leer.

As Julie showed him through the house, it was clear he had read the family history and studied his grandfather's notes. She also realized he had accepted the story of her ghostly visitation as though it were nothing extraordinary, asking her to repeat her experience while he listened gravely.

"Aren't you annoyed at whatever it is that keeps them from just telling you where the magic garden is?" he asked.

"Well, it would make things easier," she replied dryly, "but where is the fun in that?"

"I see it now; you really are enjoying all of this." He narrowed his eyes and looked at her appraisingly. "You just don't want Gustavia to know how much so you play it off, but you're into the whole thing."

"Busted." She admitted. "It was a bit scary at first—seeing ghosts, getting dragged into all this aura stuff—but who could resist a treasure hunt?"

"Then you must have some idea what you are looking for and where to find it."

"Not a clue," she said. "And it is frustrating because there are records of certain things that great-grandfather inherited; but, once he got hold of them, the documentation stops. He was secretive about his finances; so there's no telling what he might have hidden away. I don't think he had anything like a treasure chest full of gold and jewels, but there are records listing some heirloom silver and some nice pieces of jewelry. I have no idea what he did with his own money if he had any left at the end. "

"Are you thinking there might be something else?"

"There could be. Grams said the magic garden was a place of light and not to think literally. I don't know what it all means, but I doubt Gustavia will find anything, even if she dowses the entire property."

"And she probably will," they both spoke at once. Julie laughed. "You got to know her pretty well after only a day," she said.

"Gustavia is one of those rare people who open themselves up to new experiences and to new people without reservation," he said.

"You are absolutely right. I used to worry about her. People like her are so easily used by others because they are seen as superficial. Gustavia isn't like that: she has depth and an uncanny sense about people and their motives. There is a lot more to her than most people see."

"I get that," he said. "She is quite remarkable, but I suspect getting on her bad side would be a mistake."

"In more ways than one," Julie answered. "She knows Krav Maga."

Tyler burst out laughing, "That doesn't surprise me at all." A quick mental image of Gustavia in her long skirts throwing down some moves delighted him. On a more serious note, he saw an opening to bring up Logan's behavior and took it. "It looked like she wanted to use it on your fiancé today."

Julie sighed, "They don't get along at the best of times, and today was not even close to one of those." Several emotions warred inside Julie. She did not want to be disloyal to Logan, even if she was not sure at this point where the relationship stood. She also did not want to speak negatively of Gustavia; but she knew, since he had witnessed the whole fracas, Tyler deserved some explanation.

"Logan thinks Gustavia is a flake, and she finds him insufferable. She doesn't trust him and thinks he is out to get something from me. Though, what that might be, I cannot understand. All I have is this house, and it needs work—more work than I can easily afford—so I don't know what it is she thinks he is after. There's no way he knew about any kind of hidden valuables because I didn't know about them myself."

Tyler filed this information away. He intended to do some research because his gut was telling him Gustavia was correct in her assessment of Logan. If his gut was right, there must be something of value in this house— something Logan had identified long before the ghosts had verified the deathbed story of the magic garden. Whatever it was, if Logan could find it, so could he.

Testing the waters, he asked, "What if she's right? He wanted you to sign a prenuptial agreement; maybe there is something he wants, something you don't even know about."

"Maybe; I haven't had a chance to look at the papers yet. That was part of the problem earlier. He wanted me to sign them, but had not given me a copy to read first; I refused, and he got upset."

Upset didn't half cover it. Obviously, the man was up to something nefarious, but he said nothing aloud and waited for Julie to continue.

"I know it doesn't look good. It probably means Gustavia was right and great-grandfather's talk of treachery referred to those papers and to Logan. My life has gone completely out of control in the space of a couple of days." The words rushed out of Julie as she tried to make sense of all the things that had happened.

Again Tyler remained silent, letting her work it out for herself. Clearly, her best bet was to dump that jerk, but pushing right now would be counterproductive. He also needed to think about why someone he had only known for a day had already begun to matter to him, but what a day it had been.

"First things first: I am going to read over those papers tonight, and I will talk to Gram's lawyer tomorrow. After that, I'll need to do some thinking."

It was time to lighten the mood. "It's no good thinking on an empty stomach; why don't you invite me to dinner, and we can go over those notes I brought, maybe brainstorm a little. I've read through them; I don't remember anything specific about the magic garden beyond the deathbed mention, but it can't hurt to go over them again."

There was that manic glint in his eye most men get when they have visions of treasure chests dancing in their heads.

Julie recognized that glint; it was eerily similar to the one she had seen in Gustavia's eyes ever since the fateful reading. "Oh, no. Not another treasure hunting addict," she said.

"C'mon, I'm a guy. It's treasure of some sort. I think there's some sort of code I would be breaking if I didn't try to get in on this," he grinned at her, and she couldn't help but give in, "besides, my grandfather's notes tend to be a bit cryptic until you get to know his style, I can help."

"Might as well get to work then. It looks like there will be no rest around here until this mystery is resolved."

Tyler followed her into the kitchen and made himself at home. As Julie pulled ingredients from the fridge, he grabbed a knife from the block and began chopping vegetables to construct a salad while she seasoned a pair of chicken breasts and put them on the range's built-in grill. He even put together a simple, but tasty, vinaigrette to pour over the top.

From the corner Estelle watched. Now, this young man had some potential. Just look at the way they worked together, neither of them questioning the easiness of their movements around the kitchen. He set the table while she pulled a bottle of wine from the cooler and poured them each a glass. They chatted about books and movies finding they had some shared interests, but just enough differences to make things interesting. Estelle smiled. This was more like it.

After they finished eating and cleared the table, Tyler spread the notes out; they were already sorted in chronological order, so it only took a few minutes to find the sections that might contain the information they wanted.

His earlier prediction proved correct; there was nothing in the notes about a magic garden beyond the brief mention of the deathbed confession. Still, they scanned the documents for clues. At this point, any information was better than none. But all they found was another dead end.

Frustrated, Julie threw her hands up and groaned, "This is ridiculous. I have no idea what to do next. The only clue I have is that my grandmother told me not to think so literally. Ed dug up most of the property and didn't find a thing. It seems to me he would have had at least some idea what his own father might mean by a magic garden if he didn't mean a literal garden. I see ghosts regularly, my relationship is crumbling, and I have had my aura

fixed twice in just a couple of days.
What else could possibly happen next?"
She said.

"Don't tempt fate," he said, and Julie
sighed.

Maybe, Tyler thought, it was time to
leave and let Julie get her bearings. He
hoped tonight would be a more
peaceful night. She deserved it. He felt
an odd mix of protectiveness and
admiration for this woman, even
though he was sure it would irritate her
if she knew he was having these kinds
of feelings. It wasn't that he thought
she lacked strength, but he could see
she was out of her element and still
weighed down with grief over her

recent loss. It was obvious she could take care of herself; he just hoped she realized asking for help was not a sign of weakness.

As she walked him to the door, he asked, "Will you call me if anything else happens?" He saw she was thinking about saying no. "No, I mean it. You can't just dangle a treasure hunt, goddesses and fairies in front of a guy and then not let him in on the deal."

She gave in. "Okay, give me your number." Then she passed him her phone to let him enter the digits.

When he had finally gone, Julie sighed. She still had to read those infamous papers, and she was dreading it.

Chapter Twelve

Knowing what was inside the envelope would affect her future one way or another made it difficult to slide the documents out and take a look. Everything she had planned up until now depended on what was inside, and she felt as though she couldn't quite breathe. Maybe everyone would be proved wrong, and the papers would be what Logan had said, just boilerplate agreements with no sinister agenda. She hoped they would because otherwise, it meant the end of her relationship. Still, who was she kidding? The way he'd acted today, she was pretty sure it was the end anyway.

Logan hadn't been himself today, or possibly he had, and if so, that was a big problem. Somehow, his mask had slipped; if what he had shown her was his true self, she was not impressed. He had inclined to hit her; she was sure of it. Even if it was only a reaction to extreme stress, it was not a reaction she could live with. It almost seemed pointless to even open the envelope because the contents would only confirm what her heart had already begun to accept. Logan was not the man for her. Still, how could she not at least give him the benefit of the doubt?

Enough of this indecision, she thought. She could argue with herself all night.

Either way, she had to look.

Slowly she slid its contents out of the envelope and began to read. There was a lot of legalese, but there was no mistaking the intent of the prenuptial agreement. Hayward house would belong to Logan outright upon their marriage. Oh, it was all made to look like a protective measure, but the outcome was the same no matter what the intention. On her wedding day, she would lose all rights to her family home. Just as damning, the life insurance papers were not for a mutual policy, as she had expected; but one on her alone. It was a multi-million-dollar policy. Julie shivered.

Even though she knew it would be bad, she was stunned at the depth of his betrayal. There would be no need to call Grams' lawyer; the documents were clear enough. It chilled her blood to think Logan had wanted her to sign them without first reading the contents.

Thank God Gustavia had taken her to see Kat. Even if it meant changing her entire life, she was ready. Logan was about to get a surprise. Feelings of anger were beginning to edge out the pain of his betrayal. She wondered what had made him think she was stupid enough to fall for something this sleazy. She was dismayed to find he must have thought her gullible since he had taken the time to consult a lawyer before pressing her to fall in line with his scheme.

Grams had been right, and so had Gustavia; they both thought Logan was less than genuine in his feelings. Gustavia had called him a dirtbag when she didn't think Julie was listening. They both wanted the best for her, but that knowledge did nothing to provide comfort. Neither did the thought she might not have paid enough attention to the situation if her great-grandfather hadn't been so insistent. She'd trusted Logan. He'd used that trust to try and steal her legacy: even if her legacy, at the moment, was a house needing repairs that would surely land her in debt. He had nearly managed to do it, too.

That was another point to consider. As far as she knew, before today Logan had had absolutely no idea, there was any possibility of a family fortune. He'd thought the house was a liability, so his intense desire to take possession of it made no sense. Unless he knew something she didn't, there wasn't anything to be gained.

So, it was possible his intentions were good, and he had only been trying to take care of her: in a dictatorial way, to be sure; but, for the admittedly short time she had known him, Logan had mostly been kind and gentle. It was only in recent weeks he had been acting differently. Maybe he was under some kind of stress and had made a mistake in communicating with the lawyer. There could be some other explanation, though it would have to be pretty spectacular to excuse his behavior today. Still, judging him without hearing his side seemed a bit churlish even if the evidence was mounting against him.

Wearily, she resolved to put the whole thing aside and get some sleep before she gave in to the temptation to scream. Tomorrow afternoon she would talk to Logan, see what he had to say for himself.

Now if the ghosts would just leave her alone for a night.

Back at Hayward House, Julie watched Gustavia drive away more slowly than her usual mad pace. She knew Gustavia considered her family. That, like Julie, Gustavia felt like they were sisters of the heart—even if they shared no blood ties—and there was nothing one of them wouldn't do to help the other.

On the first day of sophomore year at college, Julie was nervous about meeting her new roommate. She hadn't had time to call Eloise Roman before the beginning of school, so she didn't know what to expect. Hesitantly, she entered the room then stopped dead in her tracks.

Eloise was seated inside of a pyramid made out of copper tubing with a large crystal hanging from the apex. And if that were the weirdest thing in the room, it would have been enough to freak her out; but it wasn't. More crystals dangled over the bed, along with bunches of dried herbs and flowers attached to fairy lights stapled to the ceiling in a spiral pattern, lit candles covered the dresser, the walls were hung with large batik scarves in every conceivable color and pattern. It was nearly vivid enough to make Julie's eyes water.

Eloise was wearing a long white dress that perfectly set off her hair. It was the hair that had so fiercely captured Julie's attention that she was staring open-mouthed. Dreadlocks dyed in rainbow colors was not a look you saw every day. This was going to be a disaster.

For her part, Eloise continued to sit quietly under Julie's intense scrutiny. She was used to this kind of thing. Finally, she spoke. "Hi, I'm Eloise. Well, for another week anyway; then my name will be legally changed to **Gustavia**." She arose gracefully from the center of the pyramid, tilted her head and repeated, "Hi, I'm Eloise." When there was no response, she snapped her fingers in front of Julie's eyes. This finally got her attention.

Julie stammered, "Oh, hi. Sorry, I . . . Hi. I'm Julie." She held out her hand. Then, a funny thing happened. At the touch of their hands, a warm feeling of love and acceptance washed over Julie.

She was pretty sure Eloise felt something as well because her eyes widened. Then Eloise smiled and enveloped Julie in a hug, which Julie returned, and the two began to laugh. That was the moment they knew they were soul sisters and neither would ever be alone again.

These two women were polar opposites, but it made no difference whatsoever. Julie didn't believe in all the woo-woo stuff; and Eloise, who soon became Gustavia, didn't hold that lack of enlightenment against her. Underneath the rainbow exterior beat the heart of a survivor. Her less than nurturing childhood had not soured Gustavia on life. If anything, it had the opposite effect: creating a deeply sensitive, passionately loyal person with a boundless depth of empathy. Each of these traits would have been enough to bind the friendship for life; but when Gustavia met Grams, and the two of them also clicked, she became family.

They thought of each other as sisters; and, like sisters, there were times when they bickered over one thing or another. These arguments were rare and never lasted long. Only one was never resolved: an ongoing disagreement over whether Julie should allow Gustavia to pay for the needed repairs to Hayward House. Gustavia was willing to dip into the trust fund she had vowed never to touch in order to help. There was no way Julie was going to accept that option. She knew exactly what that money meant to her friend. Using it would open old wounds, and there was no way she wanted to be linked to that kind of pain. Better to sell the house than to have Gustavia feel the need to go to her family for the money.

Her one and only interaction with Gustavia's family painted a vivid picture of what it had meant to grow up a Roman. Both parents were so caught up with the perception of their own importance that they never seemed to connect with their daughter. Beyond the indifference was also a sense of disappointment. Gustavia's parents made no attempt to understand or appreciate the uniqueness of their daughter. Instead, they abandoned her to the care of her maternal grandmother: a martinet of a woman whose disapproval of her only granddaughter went bone-deep, and the emotional scars she left were worse than any physical ones ever could have been. It was remarkable that Gustavia had learned to trust another human being and a testament to her amazing soul that she was not only able to love and trust, but to inspire those same feelings in others.

An astute judge of character, Gustavia had pinpointed Logan as a user and a sneak from day one and did not hesitate to make her opinion known. When Julie announced their engagement, Gustavia had been horrified. Realizing her open animosity was not helping, she'd called a truce while inwardly vowing to watch that moronic loser like a hawk. If he put so much as a toe out of line, she was going to do something drastic.

Now, sitting at her computer to work on her latest book – this one about a young dragon – Gustavia began to type. At least, she thought she was typing her book; but, instead, all she saw on the screen were the words danger and call him spilling down the page. Clearly, her subconscious was trying to tell her something. However, when she lifted her hands from the keys, the words continued to scroll their way down and down, endlessly repeating, until she realized there was a good chance she was not alone.

Raising her voice, Gustavia said, "Estelle, is that you?" The cursor stopped abruptly. The word **yes** appeared on her screen. Even knowing this was Grams, whom she had deeply loved, Gustavia shivered.

"Is Julie in danger?" she asked. Again, "yes." This was no surprise to Gustavia.

Given Logan's obvious dislike, she hated asking the next question. "Am I?" and the answer was, **yes**.

"I need to call Zack, don't I?" Gustavia said, frustration evident in her tone. She thought she heard a faint sigh before, again seeing the word, **yes** appear.

"Ah, Grams, you know how much I hate to do that." The sigh sounded again, no more than a whisper of breath.

"Okay, fine. But can you at least tell me where the magic garden is?" This time the answer was, **no**, followed by the feeling of a caress on her cheek; then the curtains fluttered slightly, and Gustavia knew the visitor was gone.

Many people, Logan included, made assumptions about her intelligence based on the way she dressed, her interests, and her career. It was a mistake to take Gustavia Roman at face value; she had a shrewd and calculating mind hidden under a flamboyant exterior. Her instincts were highly developed, and she was loyal to her friends. If she needed to kick some ass, she would do it without question or reservation. When Gustavia was in, she was all in.

Grumbling in protest, but determined to protect her friend, Gustavia gave in and did something that almost made her skin crawl. She called her brother.

Zack Roman was a cop. One who was considered good at his job. And, big shock, they did not get along. Zack disapproved of pretty much every one of his sister's choices: he thought she was not living up to her potential; and, except Julie—whom he considered normal—he despised all of Gustavia's friends. For her part, Gustavia was annoyed because Zack was a talented artist and, instead of following his passion, she felt he had kowtowed to their father. She never liked to see potential wasted. So, they fought nearly every time they were in the same room.

Zack was not thrilled to hear from his sister.

"What do you want? Is there a ghostly perp or did the Tarot cards tell you I was in grave danger?"

"Cut it out, Zack. This is important. It's Julie," Gustavia stated.

"Okay. I'm listening." Zack had only met Julie the one time, but he had liked her. She was the most normal friend his sister had ever brought home.

"You know she got engaged to this guy Logan, right? Well, there is something hinky about him. I think he's a con man."

"I need more to go on than just your intuition, Eloise." He refused to call Gustavia by her preferred name.

"You know I wouldn't call you unless it was important. You can pull that stick out of your backside and at least check this guy out. If it turns out there's nothing to find, which I seriously doubt, I'll let it go. But, for Julie's sake, I have to ask. You know I would never call you unless it was necessary."

Zack knew this was true; he also knew how much he wished he could feel differently about his sister. This constant animosity was difficult because underneath it there was love, even if neither could or would pull it to the surface.

"Fine, but I doubt there will be anything to find. Give me the particulars, and I'll see what I can do."

Gustavia realized she had almost no concrete information about Logan but told Zack all she could, vowing to dig deeper at her earliest opportunity. The siblings hung up, both wishing the conversation had gone better and both thinking it could have gone worse.

The conversation with Zack pointed out how little they knew about Logan's past; someone that tight-lipped must be hiding something, but what? What she needed was the inside scoop. Maybe the best way to get that was to go undercover. She called Amethyst and invited her to go on a recon mission the next day. It involved shopping. They were going incognito.

Amethyst walked into the thrift shop where she was supposed to meet Gustavia. Looking around, she didn't see her friend anywhere, so she browsed through a few racks to kill time. The only other shopper in the store was a corporate type: blond, with her hair pulled back into an elegant chignon and wearing one of those power-suit outfits. Amethyst didn't pay her much attention until, after five minutes or so, she began making a lot of noise by picking up shoes and putting them back on the rack as loudly as she could. Amethyst was beginning to get annoyed. She looked at her watch and wondered what was taking Gustavia so long. Then the power suit bimbo walked right up to her and said, "Hello." Oh my Goddess; it was Gustavia, in disguise.

"Well, look at you," Amethyst said.

Gustavia, eyes sparkling with amusement, said, "You didn't recognize me at all, did you?"

"No, I didn't," Amethyst shook her head in emphasis. "I thought you were just another one of those corporate types."

"I think I could walk right up to Logan and he wouldn't know it was me. Thankfully, I don't plan to get that close, but it is good to know I probably could. Now, it's your turn."

Amethyst gestured to her hair and eyebrows. "I don't think I can pull off that type of transformation."

"Yeah, you're going to have to wear a wig, and let's hope eyebrow pencil will cover that purple."

Amethyst looked doubtful. "A wig? Those things never look real."

"Since Logan has never met you, all you have to do is pull off a business look. He won't be looking that closely. I saw a wig behind the counter that's made from human hair; it can't hurt to at least try it."

Getting Amethyst into normal clothing took almost an hour and enough outfits to warrant a movie montage. She had a knack for finding pieces in suitable shapes, but in colors that were not remotely businesslike or, if she got the colors right, the shapes were all wrong.

First, she managed to find an '80s number in a somber navy blue that had short, puffy sleeves and a set of ridiculously huge shoulder pads. Next, she found a nice updated suit with a well-cut jacket and a pencil skirt that fit her perfectly but was a hideous shade of purple. She drooled over that one, but Gustavia vetoed it and chose a businesslike suit in chocolate brown. To assuage Amethyst's aversion to **normal-wear,** they picked out a beautiful scarf to add a bit of color. Finally, appropriately dressed and wearing the wig and makeup, they decided she would pass scrutiny. All they had to do now was drive into the city and start gathering Intel. Since Amethyst didn't own a car, they took Gustavia's making sure to park far enough away that Logan would not see it and connect it to them.

On the way into the city, Gustavia outlined her plan of attack. She had done some basic research online and come up with a cover story. She had some funds to invest and had made an appointment to talk to the head of the firm. Amethyst had an appointment with Logan. She, too, would pose as a potential client: one who was interested in hearing about properties in and around the area near Julie's home.

As they strode through the lobby with empty briefcases, both women were slightly nervous but determined to play their parts well. They wished each other luck as they took separate elevators, each one going to a different floor.

Gustavia stepped off the elevator and onto marble tile, her heels clicking all the way to the tall front desk made from dark wood polished to a gleam. Behind the desk, a young, dark-haired man professionally fielded calls and, giving Gustavia the once-over, smiled and held up one finger to indicate he would only be a minute.

Once he was off the phone, Gustavia gave him the fake name that she had used to make the appointment and was told Mr. Conti would be with her shortly. As she waited, Gustavia looked around the office. It was definitely a high-end establishment if the furnishings were any indication. In one corner was a waterfall feature surrounded by an arrangement of tropical plants. Expensive paintings hung on the wall leading to the corner office. Gustavia recognized a Picasso and a Cezanne.

The office door opened, and her heart leaped into her throat as Logan exited the room speaking over his shoulder, "I have that appointment right now; you won't be disappointed." He walked right past her as she stood in the reception area. His eyes passed right over her with no sign of recognition. It was several minutes before her heart slowed to its normal pace.

After being escorted back to Mr. Conti's office, had to hide a smile; it looked like Amethyst wasn't the only one wearing a wig today. Mr. Conti, apparently follicly challenged, wore a fairly ugly toupee. He invited her to sit and offered coffee, which Gustavia politely declined.

She followed her script emulating the cool and professional tone she had heard her parents use while growing up. It was not hard to convince the man she had investable assets. Gustavia was telling the truth, more or less. She had a trust fund; if she wanted to touch it, she would have had plenty to spend. She explained she lived north of the city and preferred to invest in her own, local area. Conti tried to steer her toward several current projects in the city until she firmly informed him if he had nothing suitable in her area, she would leave her card, and he could call her when he did.

Finally realizing she was not about to budge, he explained he did have something in the works, but the deal had not been finalized yet. He then described Julie's property stating that, once they had access to the acreage, the house would be torn down and the land developed into a high-end community of condos.

Aha, Gustavia thought. She knew it. Logan had been planning something totally shady from the beginning. Wait until she told Amethyst. She dreaded the thought of telling Julie, though.

Keeping a lid on her emotions, she asked if he had an investor's packet for the property. Then she asked who was heading up the project. Exactly as she'd suspected: it was Logan.

Gustavia wasn't sure if it was appropriate to ask for information on Logan's background in light of her prospective investment, but she did it anyway. Conti didn't seem to think this was out of the ordinary and supplied some basic details from Logan's resume, including the last place he had worked. Then she shook hands with Mr. Conti, left the office, and took the elevator down to wait for Amethyst.

She waited for what seemed like forever, but was only about ten minutes, before the elevator doors opened and she saw her friend, anger practically shooting off of her like sparks. Gustavia shook her head slightly to indicate they should not talk about their experiences until they got outside. They walked the few blocks back to the car in silence, Amethyst seething and Gustavia contemplative. How would she break the news to Julie?

Once in the car, Amethyst exploded. "That sleaze bag hit on me. And then, he tried to sell me a condo in some community they are planning to build on Julie's property. He said they would be building within the next three months; and, if I wanted in, I should leave a deposit today because the units will go fast."

"Well, now we know what he has been up to. I found out where he worked before this job. It's too bad I couldn't think of a way to get more personal information about him. I would love to see his personnel file."

Amethyst continued to rant most of the way back home while Gustavia stayed quiet. She had to tell Julie; and, even worse, she had to call her brother again and give him all the information she had found. If it helped him track Logan's past, it would be worth it because there was no way he was getting his slimy hands on Julie's home or on Julie herself, if Gustavia had her way.

Chapter Thirteen

After booting up his laptop the next morning, Tyler initiated a low-level search on Logan Ellis. Not surprisingly, all the data he found was recent. Over dinner the night before, he had used his interviewing skills to pry as much information out of Julie as he could without arousing any suspicion. Logan claimed to be from a small town in

Indiana, but there was no birth record to be found.

Until he popped up at his present job, there was no record anywhere of Logan's existence. This was not the first time he had seen this type of pattern. Tyler's biggest story to date had been an exposé on a con man who targeted the elderly, and everything about Logan was ringing the same bells in his head. So, he went a bit deeper.

Most people who learn how to lie convincingly can do so by telling at least some truth. He initiated searches throughout the entire state of Indiana for male births listing either the first name **Logan** or the last name **Ellis** and expanded the search to the year before and after the birth year Julie had given him. Those search parameters yielded better results. Now he was looking at six possibilities.

He crossmatched these with death records eliminating two from the list. Of the four remaining, two were easily located; they still lived in their home towns, were married and had children. Now, he was down to two: Logan Stewart and Kyle Ellis. His gut told him Kyle Ellis was the one; but, like any good journalist, he knew he had to verify his information.

He ran the names of both boys and their parents through public records search. Logan's parents had divorced when he was two, and his mother remarried. Her new husband adopted her son; under his adopted name, it was easy to track him to Ohio where he was now living and working.

Thornton Ellis, the man listed as Kyle's father on his birth records, was currently living in Michigan City, Indiana, a guest of Indiana State Prison. Miranda Ellis, Kyle's mother, had been looking for her son for years. She'd blogged about her search in the hope that going public might bring new leads. On her blog, she'd speculated that her ex-husband, after taking her son from her, had probably lied to keep Kyle from trying to make contact.

Tyler fired off an email to her asking for more information, but what most interested him were the photographs she had posted on her website. There was one of Thornton Ellis holding a young boy in his arms. The picture was just fuzzy enough that Tyler couldn't tell whether the boy might have grown up to become Logan Ellis or not, but the man he had met looked a fair bit like Thornton. It wasn't enough for definitive proof, but it was a good start.

Zack Roman was on a similar track. He'd begun his research by running Logan's name through the DMV records and coming up empty. He expanded his search to surrounding states with the same results; then he went nation-wide and still turned up nothing. It happened sometimes: records fell through cracks in the system, but he had to admit his sister was probably right. This guy was starting to trip a few triggers.

He scrubbed a hand over his face and sighed. He'd wanted Eloise to be wrong. It was small of him; he admitted that fact freely, if only to himself. But, just the same, he'd hoped to show her up even if it didn't make sense. Somehow, the need to score points off of her was still strong even though he was an adult.

Probably it was his own insecurity that made him unable to accept her with all of her new-age ideas, but he had a copy of every one of her books and was secretly proud of her writing ability. He knew she was successful, but he just could not overlook her lifestyle: look at the way she dressed. Her hair. She took pride in not acting anything like what he considered normal. He'd hoped Julie, being more level-headed than Eloise's other friends, would have been a better influence; but, so far, it had not happened, and he didn't think it ever would.

Drawing his attention back to the search he'd begun, Zack tried a trick that had worked for him in the past. He checked out Julie's Facebook page to see if he could find a photo of Logan. He then used the tagging feature to see if any other names might come up in conjunction with the facial recognition software the site used for images. It was a crude method, but effective. Even people on the run sometimes ended up on Facebook, making it a great resource for research. He knew of four busts already this year using the website.

Facebook tagged Logan as Ellis Thornton and also as Kyle Miranda. Each hit was another red flag. Each hit meant another reason he would have to admit to his sister her instincts had been right. Man, he hated that. He was already feeling drawn into this mess, and he was pretty sure it was going to get worse before it got better. Zack initiated the runs on both names and got up to pour himself another cup of coffee, his fourth of the day.

Ellis Thornton popped on an assault charge in Indiana. **Gotcha**, Zack thought, as he looked at the mug shot and saw a younger, rougher looking version of Logan Ellis. Ellis Thornton had been booked for assault after a bar fight that witnesses said he'd started when one of the regular patrons had called him out for manhandling a woman. Thornton had beaten the guy badly but had gotten off with community service. Kyle Miranda had a clean arrest record, though there'd been allegations he had conned some people out of some money. It had been smallish amounts each time. Since nothing could be proved, no formal charges had been filed; but Kyle had been on the radar until he vanished. It looked like he laid low for a few months and then reappeared under the name of Logan Ellis.

On a hunch, Zack crosschecked all of these names with missing persons and came up with the name **Kyle Ellis.** When he saw the names **Thornton** and **Miranda** listed as parents, he was sure he had tracked this Logan back to his roots. It took no time at all to locate Thornton Ellis in prison and Miranda Ellis by her blog. As Zack read her heart-wrenching pleas for help in finding her son, he pitied her for what she would learn if she ever did.

Zack was also sorry that he would be the one to burst her bubble. Kyle was his now, and he would not rest until he found the evidence he needed to put the man in jail where he belonged. His cop sense told him that there was plenty to find, and before it was all over, more people would come forward with evidence. Men like him always left a trail of broken marks behind.

It didn't occur to Zack that what he thought of as his cop sense was actually intuition, similar to that which his sister considered a supernatural capability if highly honed, as his was. If that concept had dawned on him, he might have allowed himself to deepen their bond; but, being pragmatic, he just assumed all cops got those feelings from time to time, and those who acted on them usually were the ones who ended up getting promoted. He had relied on his gut to get him to this position, and he intended to keep it.

Hitting print, Zack began putting together a file on Logan. Once the laser printer spat out the last of the documents, he added these to the file and marked it **personal** before slipping it into his top desk drawer. He would keep the entire thing under wraps, at least for now, because he didn't have any hard evidence; but he planned to continue digging. Then, giving in to the inevitable, he grabbed the phone and dialed his sister's number.

After telling her what he knew and hearing what she had learned, Zack read his sister the riot act for possibly putting herself and her friend in danger. He got the feeling she wasn't paying attention.

"Look, I found out what I needed to know, and nobody got hurt. He walked right past me without a hint of recognition. Everyone's fine, and now we have more information. It was a win-win."

"You think it was a good idea to put yourself in his crosshairs?"

"Oh, stop with the concerned act. We both know it's just for show."

There was silence on his end that stretched out until he spoke quietly, "That's not fair, and it's not true."

"From where I'm sitting, it is. Can we just leave our own crap out of this?"

"Fine, but this isn't over."

When Gustavia ended the call, she just sat still for a moment. A feeling of vindication flooded her; she had been right all along: Logan was a creep and a con man. Next came a wave of sadness. Julie was about to lose another person from her life; and, even if it was all for the best, Gustavia knew it would hurt her friend.

She wasn't quite sure what her next step should be. Zack had explained that finding Logan's aliases was not enough; he needed hard evidence to prove Logan was guilty, and at this point, the only thing he could prove was the man had changed his name. Zack pointed out that Eloise had done the same thing; it was not a crime. As of right now, there were no warrants against either of those aliases.

Zack had asked his sister not to say anything to Julie until there was more information, but this did not sit right with Gustavia. Julie needed to be protected before Logan managed to get her to sign something that would cost her everything she owned. That wasn't even the worst of it: Julie needed to know so she could protect her heart.

So, Gustavia had given her brother one week. Then she was going to talk to Julie and hope that, by waiting, she would not lose her sister and best friend.

Chapter Fourteen

As it turned out, Gustavia did not have to wait the full week to come clean with Julie because, three days later, Logan managed to take care of the problem himself.

Julie had spent the morning finalizing the jewelry shots for Tamara. They didn't need much more than a few tweaks, so she was able to run them in batches through Camera Raw. The whole process only took a couple of hours. After she was finished with those, she opened up the files from the kaleidoscope mirror images for evaluation. They were good, but there was something missing, so she printed several of them out. This was part of her process: when an image or series wasn't quite working, she often printed out a few and tacked them to the wall. This let her live with them a few days until she got a new inspiration.

She was pinning the last one to the board when her phone rang. It was Tyler.

"Invite me to lunch," he said.

"What?"

"Invite me to lunch; I promise it will be worth it."

"I'm just finishing up some work; but, okay, let's do lunch." Her doorbell rang. Still carrying the phone, she opened the door, and there he was, a huge grin on his face, a large bag in hand. Smiling in welcome, she hung up the phone and gestured for him to come in. Tyler waved the bag saying,

"It's fried chicken, my mother's recipe. C'mon, picnic in the gazebo," and he led Julie out the back door and across the lawn toward the formal garden.

Tyler unpacked the picnic lunch while Julie went back to the house for lemonade and utensils. Making a decided effort to keep the conversation light, Tyler asked Julie about her work. The one room she had not shown him during the tour was her studio.

He had not yet decided whether to tell Julie about his research on Logan. It was a tricky subject. He was well aware that since he had only known her for a short time, she was apt to find his interest meddlesome, but he couldn't help himself. He liked this woman. Even if he was over-stepping his bounds, he still felt this nagging need—almost like a voice in his ear—to keep an eye on her.

And, speaking of the devil, Julie's relaxed posture went noticeably tense. Tyler turned to see Logan striding toward the gazebo, followed by Gustavia who had apparently arrived at the same time.

"Should I take off?" Tyler asked Julie in a low voice.

"No," she answered, "you might as well stay. I don't think this is going to take long." Somehow, she felt comfortable enough with him that his presence did not feel like an invasion of privacy; but instead, it felt supportive, comforting, right. Gustavia, long legs flashing, passed by Logan to reach Julie first and gave her a big hug while whispering in her ear, "Be careful; he seems unstable." Julie could see that for herself.

There was something different about Logan today. It was as though more of the wall between his inside and his outside had eroded to reveal a little more of the man, the monster underneath. He was making an effort to smile and appear genial, but he wasn't quite able to quell the cold glint in his eyes and the slight curling of his lip that spoke of the seething anger just below the surface. Julie felt his contempt, and it shocked her. She had been prepared to give him the benefit of the doubt; but, now, most of her willingness washed away as Logan greeted Gustavia, again flashing that look of hatred Julie had glimpsed the day before. She waited for him to speak.

"I only have a few minutes. So if you would go and get those papers, I can drop them off at the lawyer's on my way back to the city," he spoke as though her signing the documents was a foregone conclusion.

"I'm sorry, Logan; but I haven't signed anything." She was waiting for an explanation of their contents or some sign that would tell her what his intent had been when he had them drawn up. She was holding out to give him that final chance, and she was quickly losing hope.

"Look, Julie, I can't waste any more time on this. If we are going to be married, we need to have our financial affairs in order. I can't accept anything less."

Julie's stomach flipped once, then twice, then began to feel hollow.

"I am never going to sign those papers; you need to drop this right now. It is not an option. My great-grandfather warned me about them, and he was right," Julie spoke forgetting she had decided not to tell Logan about her ghostly visits.

He stared at her for what felt like a long time, "Your dearly departed great-grandfather? You cannot be serious.

Exactly how did he manage to communicate from beyond the grave? Did you go to a séance or maybe he left you a message on a fogged up mirror in the bathroom? C'mon, Julie. Don't be some sort of new-age cliché."

"It's not a cliché, Logan. I saw my great-grandfather—he and Grams both, to be exact—in the library the other night. He warned me not to sign any papers, and he was right. I read them. They give you ownership of everything. Complete ownership, Logan," She repeated it again for emphasis, "Sole ownership of my family home. I would like some explanation."

Logan said nothing; Julie realized, if he'd had a reason, he didn't plan to share it with her. That couldn't be good. Far from the devastation, she should have been feeling, indignation flashed to the surface as her hands ached to clench into fists.

"Well? Do you have an excuse? Quite frankly, I think your refusal to answer says a lot about your motives."

Brushing off any acknowledgment of treachery, Logan tried to shift the focus. "That idiot Gustavia's been putting ideas in your head. Seeing dead people. Why would you want to continue spending time with her, anyway?" Logan asked. "She's crazy; and, if you aren't careful, it will rub off on you."

"Gustavia is not crazy, and neither am I. I know what I saw. Leave her out of this and answer the question." Julie was incensed; he would say something so nasty right in front of her friend. She was even more irked he offered no explanation, no excuse, not a word in his own defense. She had expected him to have something positive to say for himself, but there was nothing. Her heart sank as she realized the misgivings she had been having were justified. Grams shimmered next to her, unseen. Her plan was working.

"It's time you grew up and stopped holding on to your college days." He practically spat the words in her direction. "Time to make new friends, the right kind of friends. You have a degree in art history; why do you waste your time with those little photographs when you could be working in a museum? We need to go to the lawyer, get those papers signed, and move up the wedding date. It is time you had someone to take care of you, teach you how to make better choices."

"So basically, what you are saying is every decision I ever make in my life is a bad one. From the friends I choose to my career, I always get it wrong?"

"Well, that's a little harsh, don't you think? I wouldn't go that far, but you have made more than your fair share of mistakes," he replied as though realizing he had stepped over a line.

"I think the only mistake I made was accepting your proposal, to begin with. That is one mistake I can rectify quite easily. The engagement is off; the wedding is off, and I never want to see you again!" She pulled the ring from her finger and hurled it at him.

Rage flashed through him, hot as a fiery furnace. No one confronted him. No one ever questioned his motives. No mark had ever screwed up one of his cons until now. His face burned with anger, and he grabbed her by the arm. Hard. Hard enough to leave a series of finger marks. Then he bent, retrieved the ring, and tried to jam it back on her finger as she stood, dumbfounded, for a moment before responding.

Tyler took a step forward; it was one thing to watch them argue, another entirely to stand by while Logan shoved Julie for the second time in his presence. He clenched his hand into a fist; but before he could take another step, Julie wrenched herself out of Logan's grasp, then moved away from him, chest heaving with anger.

Furious she would dare to stand up to him, he took a half step toward her, hand raised: the intention to hit her plain on his face and in his body posture.

But half a step was all he managed. It was as though an invisible barrier rose up between them and he was unable to get any closer. There was a faint shimmer in the air near him. He struggled, his open hand quickly turning to the fist he now wanted to use to bend her will to his selfish desire. Instead of getting near enough to hit Julie, his fist raised then slammed into his own face. Hard. Shocked beyond belief, Logan stopped dead in his tracks, and all the color drained from his face. He appeared to be listening to something only he could hear, then turned on his heel and walked away.

Twice on his way across the lawn, he looked back over his shoulder at the group with a look of incredulity, but he did not stop. Getting into his car, he fishtailed down the drive.

Tyler and Gustavia looked at each other for a split second; each of them had come to the same conclusion. Logan had just had an encounter with Julie's great-grandfather. They hurried over to Julie, who was still rooted to the same spot. Even before they got close, they could see she was shaking.

When she turned around, they realized it was not fear or anger causing the tremors. Julie, tears running down her face, was laughing.

"Oh my God," she said, "why did I never see it before? He is such a total loser." It was never a good idea to agree with that type of character assessment when there was even the smallest chance it would come back to bite you in the butt, so Tyler and Gustavia both kept silent.

"Did you see that?" Julie continued on, "Tell me you saw that."

"What did you see?" Gustavia asked.

"It was great-grandfather; he somehow made Logan punch himself."

Julie continued to laugh; Gustavia began to smile. Tyler was still thoughtful; he didn't think this business with Logan was over, not by a long shot. But eventually, as both girls devolved into full out belly laughs, he was able to put aside his concern and join in.

"Did you see the look on his face?" Gustavia hooted. "It was priceless."

Julie tried to feel bad for laughing over the ending of her engagement. She fully expected she would feel bad later; but just at this moment, whether it was nerves or a genuine reaction to the situation, it felt great to laugh. She couldn't remember the last time she'd felt this lighthearted.

Eventually, the three sobered up. Gustavia knew it was time to tell Julie of her adventure and of Zack's research. She chose her words carefully.

"Julie, I have to tell you something, something about Logan; and I don't think you are going to like it," she began.

Julie steeled herself for whatever was coming.

"Logan is a con man."

"I know you've never liked him; with what just happened, I guess I have to admit you might be right."

"No, Julie, it isn't just one of my feelings. Zack checked him out, and Amethyst and I did some....well, we did a recon mission."

"A what now?" Julie asked while Tyler looked at Gustavia with renewed admiration.

"Well, we went to his office. Ammie talked to him; he gave her a spiel and tried to sell her on a condo that was going to be built here on this property."

"Gustavia, he must have recognized you; you don't exactly blend into the crowd."

"Well--we went incognito."

A range of emotions played across Julie's face, first shock, then admiration, then a wide grin of appreciation.

"Incognito?" she asked.

"Yeah, we went to the thrift store and bought suits—you know, regular clothes—and Ammie found a wig that looked real. She even colored her eyebrows."

An even bigger grin played across Julie's face.

"Movie montage?"

Gustavia beamed; it was going to be okay.

"Well, maybe a little one."

"Video footage? Please tell me there was video footage," Tyler chimed in.

Gustavia cued up the image library and passed him her phone. No video, but there were several shots of both of them in their power suits. He handed the phone to Julie, who just shook her head then wearily rubbed a hand across her eyes.

"Okay, so he had plans for the property. That makes him a bit sleazy, but does it actually make him a con man?"

Gustavia sighed, "No, but since Logan Ellis isn't his real name, and Zack found two more aliases, and he was already selling condos built on your land, it doesn't look good."

She went on, "I'm sorry I went behind your back, but Estelle visited me and told me we were both in danger."

"You've seen Grams? And you didn't tell me?" Julie asked, hurt.

"Not **seen** exactly, but she was there; she typed on my computer."

It was a lot to take in, but Julie knew Gustavia had only been trying to help; and if she had contacted Zack, the situation was serious.

"Serious enough to get Zack involved?"

Since Gustavia had eclipsed anything Tyler could add from his research, he wisely kept quiet about his own findings. He did, however, ask "Who's Zack?"

"He's Gustavia's brother—he is also a cop—and they don't have a good relationship."

"Wait, I know him; Zack Roman, right? He's a stand-up guy. Isn't his father a senator? So that would make Gustavia...." He trailed off.

"Yep," she answered, "that makes me the senator's black sheep of a daughter. Now you know my deepest, darkest secret," she teased. "Reveal it at your peril." Her exaggerated scowl failed to be fierce or menacing.

"Tyler is an investigative reporter," Julie informed Gustavia.

"So, are you going to out me to the world? It's not like I'm in hiding or anything; I just don't associate with my family by mutual agreement," Gustavia explained to Tyler.

"Your secret is safe with me," he said.

Gustavia patted his hand gently.

"It's no secret, really; I just try to stay out of the limelight when it comes to the circumstances of my birth. Zack is a good person. Everyone in my family is a good person, as long as they are dealing with normal. I don't qualify for normal, so they disapprove."

Empathy flooded Tyler's face as he took Gustavia's hand and spoke from his heart.

"They gave you a hard time; that's easy to see. But if your family doesn't see how special you are, they don't deserve you. I can tell you have family in Julie."

Gustavia bowed her head at his simple acceptance, then lifted her face with its shining smile and kissed him on both cheeks. The moment was over, and it was time to make some decisions.

"Yes, Julie is my family. I'm going to move in here for a while to make sure she stays safe."

"I was thinking of doing the same thing myself; maybe we could trade off," Tyler answered.

Julie looked from one of them to another, not sure whether to be thankful or exasperated and settled finally on a mix of the two. She opened her mouth to protest, but the words died before they could pass her lips. She was looking at identical attitudes of defiance: two sets of crossed arms, two heads slightly tilted, and two pairs of eyes dead set and just daring her to argue. Clearly, she might as well give in with some grace and dignity because nothing she could say would deter these two from their decision.

She sighed and shrugged her shoulders in acceptance.

Gustavia changed the subject.

"But tonight, I think a girl's night out is in order. Some drinks, maybe some dancing. Get your mind off of all this for a little while. You know we are way overdue." Before Julie could protest, Gustavia shot off a text. "I'm inviting Ammie and Kat; I think it is time you got to know them better."

Tyler figured if he just kept his mouth shut, he could tag along. Girls night out sounded fun; and, with this group, it was bound to be interesting. He suggested a club that offered live band Karaoke, partly because one of his friends was in the band and partly because it always proved entertaining. When the singers were good, they were very good; and when they were bad, it was even more fun.

Before Julie had time to protest, plans were made. They all finished off the picnic meal before she headed back to the house to finish up her interrupted work, then get ready for the evening. She realized her friends were just trying to protect her and keep her mind off of Logan and she appreciated their kindness more than she could say, but it was frustrating to feel like she was losing control of her own life. She would let them have this evening and even accept house guests with a modicum of grace, but there were going to have to be some limits.

Tyler went home, and Gustavia left to pack a bag for her first night on guard duty and get ready for the evening out. They assumed, rightly, that Logan would not dare show his face here again today; and Gustavia wanted to give Zack an update.

Julie was alone, probably for the last time until this whole mess got resolved.

She let herself sink into the painful feelings of another loss. Even if Logan had turned out to be a bad person, she cared about the man she thought he had been, at least for a while.

Slumped on the sofa, Julie let the tears flow until she felt a gentle touch on her shoulder. She jumped and swiftly turned to see Grams sitting next to her. "It's not nice to sneak up on a person like that; you scared me," Julie said.

"I'm sorry; I'm not quite used to being dead yet," Estelle replied. "I don't make noise unless I concentrate."

Julie just looked at her grandmother. Not all of her pain and anger was with

Logan; this whole situation was a bit overwhelming, and Grams was part of it. "So, have you come to say **I told you so** or just to pass on more cryptic messages about danger or the family fortune?" She asked, clipped tone revealing her deep frustration.

"I'm sorry you're upset, but I am glad you found out what kind of man Logan is. I won't apologize for it. He is going to be angry when he finds out his past has been discovered. Watch out for him; he is the kind of man who might strike back."

Julie nodded; she had figured that out for herself today.

"As to the family fortune, there are things I'm not allowed to tell you. This is your puzzle, but your friends will help you, and you need to let them. They love you, you know. Almost as much as I do."

The annoyance left Julie in a rush of love for her grandmother.

"I know they do."

"And Tyler seems to be fitting in well with the group. He has such a warm soul, not like that cold fish."

"Matchmaking, Grams? Really? It's only been an hour since I was an engaged woman." Julie couldn't contain her smile. Grams had always had a way of lightening a moment. "Besides, I think Gustavia's the one he is interested in."

Shaking her ghostly head, Estelle replied, "No, I don't think so, not by the way he looks at you. One thing I can tell you is this: Gustavia has an ordeal ahead of her before she finds true love."

Julie hoped not; Gustavia deserved something easy in her life.

"Logan tried to make you feel incompetent; it was one of his tools to try and control you. Remember this: you mustn't think it was because of any failing in you. Don't close yourself off again. You're young; it's time to throw caution to the wind."

Intrigued, Julie began to ask a question, but Grams just smiled and faded away.

Gustavia called Zack and told him about Logan's recent activities, leaving out any reference to ghostly interference since she knew exactly what his reaction would be to that information.

Zack hung up the phone and, deciding it was time to pull in some help, made a call to the detective who had investigated Logan's last alias. The two of them agreed to exchange information, and Zack set the wheels in motion to make the case official.

Chapter Fifteen

As he drove back to Hayward House, Tyler was thinking, all things considered, it was shaping up to be a fine day. He was headed to a bar with four head-turning women, and Julie had spectacularly dumped her complete tool of a fiancé. Now, why did that make him so happy?

Gustavia had already returned to Julie's house, and they had made plans to pick everyone else up on the way. Tyler would be driving since his vehicle was big enough to hold the whole group comfortably.

As they entered the bar, the group drew plenty of attention. Gustavia, in a floaty top, had exchanged her usual calf-length skirt for a mini that showed off a truly great set of legs. Amethyst wore a purple, polka-dotted dress that looked like something out of the sixties; the outfit completed with a pair of purple go-go boots. Kat wore black skinny jeans and a tank top covered in silver sequins. And Julie attracted plenty of attention in a form-fitting, electric-blue dress. It hugged her curves, skimmed over her butt, and showed off a lot of leg. She had done something with makeup that made her eyes look deep and mysterious.

They snagged a table and ordered drinks just as the band was introduced. It was a fun concept: instead of singing with a mike and teleprompter, wannabe singers could get a taste of what it felt like to be a real front man or woman. Tyler's friend Colby played lead guitar. The whole concept had been his idea, born out of necessity one Wednesday night when the bar was slow. Their lead singer had quit an hour before they were supposed to go onstage. In the old showbiz tradition that the show must go on, Colby asked the crowd if there was anyone who had ever wanted to sing with a band but had never had the chance. He pronounced this was Karaoke with a twist and got enough takers to fill out the entire evening. Everyone loved it, and word of mouth had turned it into a regular event.

Conversation was lively during the break after the first set with everyone discussing which had been their favorite singers. Drinks, sent by hopeful patrons, arrived regularly at the table. Tyler, as designated driver, responsibly sticking to soft drinks.

Instead of the quiet, brooding Julie he had expected to see tonight, she was lively and animated. "Why don't you take a turn at the mike," she teased Tyler. When at first, he declined, she said, "C'mon, I dare you. Chicken?"

"I will if you will, but I bet there is no way that will happen," he replied.

"What makes you so sure?"

"You just don't seem the type."

Julie raised one eyebrow, then turning to Gustavia, gave her a look. Tyler realized something was up; it was possible she was going to call his bluff.

As the band headed back to the stage, Colby stopped by the table to greet his friend and get an introduction to the four women. As he left the table,

Julie stood up and accompanied him back toward the stage. It was clear she had asked him a question when he grinned and nodded.

Colby's band took the stage, the drummer pounding out the opening beat to Joan Jett's **Do You Wanna Touch**. Julie strode out on stage, grabbed the mike and belted out the lyrics. Tyler's mouth dropped open, and his eyes nearly fell out of his head. She was good, really good. Then he heard Gustavia say, "Oh, what the heck." Leaving the table, she mounted the stage, walked up to Colby and motioned for him to hand her the guitar. Slinging the strap over her shoulder, she barely missed a beat before taking over the lead.

"Well, they can't have all the fun," said Amethyst to Kat. "Wanna?" And receiving a smiling nod, she guided Kat to take over for the bass player while she nudged the drummer out of the way. Julie looked surprised, then delighted. The four girls rocked it out. Gustavia nailed the lead; Kat played a strong bass line; and Amethyst never missed a beat, all while singing backup to Julie's vocals. Once Tyler got over the shock, he couldn't hold back a grin as the ousted band members took the empty seats at his table enjoying the show.

Julie sounded amazing; and she didn't just stand there and sing the song, she performed it. She danced and shimmied around the stage, commanding the attention of the entire room. She had the moves and the voice.

Then she slithered her way over to Tyler and, with a murderous glint in her eye, began singing straight to him. Rolling her body suggestively, she pulled him from the chair and into a short but sexy dance, then shoved him back down in his seat, turned her back emphatically and returned to the stage. Tyler wasn't sure whether to laugh or cry at this point.

When the song ended, the bar erupted in thunderous applause; then began chanting, demanding more. No one wanted the four to leave the stage. Looking at the band members now seated at their table, Julie saw their delighted expressions as they waved to indicate the women should do another number.

After a short conversation, they launched into **Rolling in the Deep** by Adele. Halfway through, Julie caught Tyler's eye and winked. He responded with the I'm-not-worthy bow and just grinned at her. This was not the little repressed wallflower he thought he had come to know. This was a raging, sexy woman in full control of her life. Where had she been all this time?

Turning the stage back over to Colby and his band, the four friends returned to the table. Laughing and excited, they enjoyed the rest of the second set. As soon as the band went on break, Tyler looked at Julie and said, "Where in the world did that come from?" She smiled triumphantly and shot a sideways look at Gustavia. "Rock Band came out during our junior year at college; we were sort of addicted. Gustavia already knew how to play acoustic guitar, so she always played lead, and I sang." Leaning forward she added, "We performed in the park sometimes for extra spending money."

She gestured toward Amethyst and Kat saying, "But these two, I had no idea they played."

"Yeah," Amethyst answered, "the three of us jam with Mishka every so often. You should come to the next session and sing lead; Mishka does it now, but she would much rather do backup."

"That sounds fun," Julie replied. Then, looking at Tyler with a glint in her eye, challenged him, "It's your turn now; a bet is a bet."

Knowing he was on the hook, Tyler relented, smiling at the entire table. The evil glint was now in his eye as he approached Colby. When the band retook the stage, it was with Tyler at the mike singing **Lonely Boy** by the Black Keys. Now it was Julie's turn to enjoy the performance, and she did. It was also her turn to look at him in a new light. He was quick-witted, kind, honest and entertaining to be with. She hadn't had this much fun in what seemed like forever.

She hadn't realized how isolated she had been during her relationship with Logan. Other than an occasional movie or dinner, they had rarely gone out and never with a group of friends. Looking back she could see that under the guise of accommodating his work schedule and his distaste for Gustavia, he had actively set her apart. Julie knew she could also blame some of it on the loss of her grandmother, but she truly hadn't realized how lonely she'd been during the past few months. Now that she saw things more clearly, she was more thankful than ever that Gustavia had not allowed him to run her off: her friend, her sister, her savior.

She was well rid of that jackass, but she couldn't shake the feeling he might not be gone for good. He'd thought she was a good mark, thought he could make her feel small and unable to care for herself. He didn't know who he was dealing with. At that moment, she resolved if he ever did come back, he would regret it. Julie lifted her head, feeling empowered again for the first time in months.

Amethyst, who was watching the play of emotions across Julie's aura, saw this moment of change; then, smiling in approval, poked Gustavia and nodded her head subtly toward Julie. Gustavia's eyes widened as she took in the changes, then her face broke out in a wide grin. It was going to be okay. Then, noticing the way Tyler was looking at Julie, she decided maybe it was going to be better than okay.

Chapter Sixteen

The ride home was full of talk and laughter. There was an ease to the conversation Julie hadn't felt for months, even when it turned to talk of ghosts and treasure, which, considering recent events, it was bound to do.

"What kind of valuables do you think you're looking for?" Amethyst asked.

"Well," Julie replied, "great-grandfather inherited some silver, and there was also some jewelry. Then, by all accounts, he made a lot of money from his first invention, but everyone thought he had probably blown it all on more inventions."

"And no idea where or what the magic garden might be?" Tyler said.

"They said not to think so literally, but I'm not sure what they meant, and they don't seem to be able to give us any other clues. Since I am not sure where to look next, I think it's probably a lost cause," Julie replied.

"What we need is a clue to help us find a clue," Gustavia stated, "or a good barnstorming session."

At that Kat cracked up, "You mean **brainstorming**, I assume."

"Yeah, isn't that what I said?" Gustavia asked.

"Not a bad idea, though. Julie, may we storm your barns?" Amethyst asked. Tyler glanced in the rearview mirror and saw the gleam in her eye.

"What do you mean? There are some outbuildings, but there are no barns on the property."

"I mean, let's all go to your house and put our heads together. Kat can do her touchy-feely thing; I can turn on my woo-woo vision; Gustavia can apply her prodigious intuition, and Tyler can..."

"Drive the Scooby van?" He asked dryly. "I have other skills, you know."

Kat waggled an eyebrow and said, "Well, we know you can stand around looking pretty, and you can sing, what else can you do?"

"He also makes a nice tossed salad with homemade dressing, and he fries a mean chicken," Julie said.

Tyler pretended to be wounded by their lack of respect; but, with visions of slumber party pillow fights in his head, he was not planning to be left out. He glanced over at Julie to see how she was taking the possibility of a full-scale assault on her privacy. He had expected her to protest, but instead, he could see she was touched by the willingness of the group to help.

"Are you okay with the idea, Julie?" Gustavia asked. She also knew Julie might be easily overwhelmed after the week she had just put in.

"Sure, why not," was the answer, "I have no idea where to look, and I would welcome the help; though I'm pretty sure we will be chasing the undomesticated goose."

At that, Ammie honked like a goose, and they all hooted with laughter.

When they got to Julie's house, the first order of business was to raid her closet for comfy clothes for all of the girls. Then they all hit the kitchen for a snack before the brainstorming began.

Tyler was way ahead of them and, after poring through the cupboards and fridge, had set out a variety of crisp veggies, crackers, cheese, and chips, along with the ever-present pitcher of lemonade Julie always seemed to have at the ready.

He had grabbed his laptop from the car. While they all munched, he began organizing what they already knew, dropping it into a mind-mapping program. This was a technique he used in his work and one he thought would serve them well; then he listed the skills each person brought to the table:

Gustavia had a keen instinct for putting things together, and she was still carrying her dowsing rods around in her bag; Kat might be able to shed some light on any nuances she picked up while channeling the ghosts, Amethyst thought she might be able to perceive aura imprints in the house, Julie would provide knowledge of the history and the house; he would organize the information.

It was a good plan.

The next question was where to start; the library or her great-grandfather's bedroom were the likeliest places, so they all trooped upstairs, Gustavia tucking Kat's hand under her arm and murmuring information about the stairs, rugs and any other tripping hazards. Since the library was the first of the two rooms, that is where they began.

"I think I should sit in the chairs where your grandparents sat the other night; I might pick up some residual energy from them," Kat said. Julie pointed them out, and Gustavia guided the psychic to the seat where Julius had been sitting.

"What should we be doing?" Tyler whispered a little too loudly.

"Nothing special. Maybe be quiet for a minute or two," Kat answered with a grin.

"Okay, I can handle that." The comment set off a round of feminine eye rolling.

While Kat was concentrating, Amethyst strolled quietly around the room, head tilting first left, then right. Several times she stopped and squinted at an area before moving on. She paid special attention to the old black walnut desk that was polished to a shine, even getting down on her knees to peer under it; but she walked right past the shimmer in the corner without noticing. Julie shifted her feet several times, not completely comfortable with the scrutiny; but still highly curious about what might happen next. Maybe they would turn up a clue, maybe they would just end the day feeling silly; either way, she was willing to go with it.

Looking over her shoulder, Julie realized Tyler was also watching, his blue eyes twinkling and a huge grin on his face. He had certainly managed to get himself deeply involved in her life over a few short days. It was the treasure hunt; like he said, no red-blooded male could resist one. She chuckled to herself. Maybe she should start a dating service that involved a treasure hunt; it would sure pull in the guys. Dating service? Where had that idea come from?

Gustavia watched Tyler; watched Julie; watched Tyler watching Julie, and Gustavia knew it was not the treasure hunt that drew him back to Hayward House; he just didn't know it yet. His eyes kept being drawn back to her friend and Gustavia revised that impression: he did know it, no way he didn't. She smiled; this relationship was going to be fun to watch. You didn't have to know Tyler long to realize he was the kind of guy who stuck like glue when he wanted something. And it was easy to see he wanted Julie.

"Oh," Amethyst exclaimed at the same time Kat's head dropped to her chest. Walking to join the other three she whispered, "her aura just totally changed; something is going to happen." She was right.

Kat lifted her head; Julie's heart leaped into her chest and began to pound as those familiar gray eyes sought hers again. **Oh, my giddy aunt**, she thought. **Grams was here earlier; I saw her with my own eyes. That didn't wig me out; but this, this is just downright creepy**. Behind her, she heard Tyler's swift intake of breath and figured he had just noticed the eyes, but he said nothing.

"Whoa." Amethyst breathed the word on a sigh while Gustavia just kept grinning. Gram's features settled gently over the mediums' in that eerie double exposure way as finally, she spoke.

"Well, hello, everyone; it's nice to see you here helping Julie. She is lucky to have such people in her life."

"Hey, Estelle. Nice to see you," Gustavia said warmly, "I've missed you."

"And I, you. I love you more than I can say, never forget that."

Kat/Estelle shifted her gaze to Amethyst and Tyler saying, "I don't think we've met."

Julie performed introductions thinking this entire situation was becoming more and more surreal by the day as her grandmother greeted her new friends.

"I am only sorry I cannot properly greet the generous child who has allowed me the opportunity for this visit. But maybe I can repay a little of her kindness. Please give her this message for me. Tell her **blue eyes will meet brown eyes, and she will know them by their color**."

Julie sighed. "More cryptic messages, more riddles. Not especially helpful, Grams." Caught somewhere between frustration and respect, Julie wanted to scream; but held her emotions in check.

For once, Tyler had little to say, no glib remark, nothing. He did comfort himself by thinking he had managed to not just stand there with his mouth hanging. At least not long enough for anyone else to notice.

Grams sighed. "I know, and I wish I could be more helpful. All I can do is tell you my firsthand account of the day he died, could we go to his rooms?"

It was a quiet group that walked down the hall, not least because Kat led the way and it was obvious her eyes were working perfectly. Julius' suite consisted of a sitting room with a small bathroom off to the left and a bedroom to the right. Off the sitting room was a balcony that, during the day, would present quite a view of the property. Most of the wall opposite the balcony was taken up by the fireplace with its ornately carved mantel which housed several family photographs and some mechanical trinkets. Above the fireplace hung a mirror that was not quite large or imposing enough for the size of the space it occupied; around its perimeter was a darker band of wallpaper indicating something larger had hung there at one time.

The bedroom was decorated in a spare, yet functional, manner with storage provided by a large wardrobe and a medium-sized dresser. The simple, metal framed bed sat in the middle of the far wall flanked by a small table on each side. On the wall to the left of his bed was one of the famed stained glass windows; the large floral scene, totally at odds with the rest of the furnishings, dominated the room. Plainly, Julius had had his way with the decorating because other than that floral window, there was no other feminine touch in any of the rooms he had shared with his wife.

As they passed Tyler's open briefcase on the desk, he grabbed the voice recorder he used for interviews. It was the best way he knew to be sure he had an accurate record of whatever Estelle had to say.

"Once he was gone, we put things back to rights; and, after that, Mary Lou never changed a thing. She kept it as a shrine after he died." They were led into the bedroom where Kat sat down on the bed. "It was here in this bed that he sat up with the firelight glittering in his eyes, stared over our heads and said, **Use the key with the magic garden; they will show you the hiding place. Follow the light**. Then he looked right at me and said, **Don't forget: key--magic garden**. He was upset, agitated. At the time I thought it was just restlessness. In his last weeks, he was in a considerable amount of pain, and his muscles twitched a lot, but I think he was gesturing toward something to his left."

Kat's head began to fall forward again and, before anyone could utter another word, Grams was gone. Gustavia sprang into action, kneeling before her friend, chafing her cold hands and talking to her in a soothing voice. She knew the psychic had been scared the last time this happened, and she was going to make sure this time was different. As Kat lifted her head, eyes once more vacant and unseeing, everyone breathed a sigh of relief to see she appeared relaxed and confident.

Still, everyone remained quiet until they were all back downstairs, comfortably seated on the vintage, but still solidly-built, sofa and chairs. Gustavia had gone to the kitchen to round up a bottle of wine and some glasses, thinking they needed something a bit stronger than lemonade after that experience.

Quiet up until now Tyler, who had been typing at a furious rate on his laptop, finally looked up and opened the conversation.

"Well," he said hesitantly, "Is everyone okay?"

Satisfied with the nods and quietly voiced affirmatives, he let out a **whoop** that managed to make every one of the women jump in their seats. "That was amazing." Nearly shouting, he got up to pace around the room excitedly before leaning down to take Kat's face in his gentle hands and plant a smacking kiss on both cheeks. "You were amazing," he told the now blushing psychic.

"I'm not exactly sure how all this stuff works, Kat; could you hear anything while it...while she..." Julie trailed off, not quite sure if the question was appropriate or not.

"Yes, I heard everything. I felt—this is hard to explain—but I felt she was sure the information was important, but not why, and she is just as frustrated about this whole thing as you are. Julius knows and can't tell anyone, not even her, where to find the secret." Then Kat provided a single clue. "She kept thinking about two things: one was a book—I could see it clearly—not a large book, blue with gold writing;

and the other was the painting of your great-grandfather."

Julie and Tyler looked at each other; it was that family history again. They had been over that thing with a fine-toothed comb and found nothing helpful. Obviously, they were going to have to read it again.

"Isn't anyone going to ask me if I saw anything?" Ammie asked with a wicked grin. "I mean really, someone channels one little spirit and no one remembers the aura reader."

Laughing, they ordered her to spill her guts.

"Well, most readers only see auras around living, breathing things. A few of us sometimes also see them around objects. When someone handles an object with strong feelings of intention, I sometimes see the object's aura with the faint echo of the human aura attached to it. Sort of like a double rainbow, but not. I know it might not make sense, but that's the best way to describe it.

"So, did you see a double rainbow?" Eyes alight, Gustavia had to ask.

"Why, yes, I did." Amethyst was delighted to be able to add some useful information. She'd begun to care about Julie, and more than anyone in the room understood how much worry the woman was carrying. Her aura told the story, even if she tried not to burden her friends with it.

Chapter Seventeen

While Julius sat watching with interest, Logan raged through his apartment like a two-year-old having a temper tantrum. It would have been funny if throwing a fit helped release his pent up anger, but it seemed to be intensifying it instead. A vase shattered against the wall followed by the half-full glass of single malt scotch. He muttered imprecations punctuated by growls of **witch** and **who does she think she is dealing with** and **I'm the one who decides**. Julius was disgusted. Real men did not act like spoiled children. Then again, real men did not try to cheat a woman out of her land or consider physical violence.

Logan was considering all kinds of physical violence. Against Julie; against Gustavia; and, now that he had finally registered his presence, against whoever that man was who kept hanging around. Probably some dweeb who was banging the freaky chick. He would show them all. Nobody screws around with a Thornton.

With an effort, he began the process of calming himself enough to think. The beast inside had nearly broken free, and that would have been a bad thing. He needed to be lucid, to take stock and see what he could salvage of the situation. That business of hitting himself in the face--that had been just weird. Never before had he taken his anger out on himself like that. It was the only explanation. There was just no other way it could have happened. No, no other way.

At that thought, Julius chuckled. The boy had gotten a taste, but that was all. Let him try to hurt Julie again and see what happened.

Finally, settled enough to sit, Logan sipped from a fresh glass of scotch and closed his eyes to think. He needed a plan B. After today, he didn't think Julie would take him back, so the wedding was a non-starter and no wedding meant she wasn't going to just sign the house over to him. Maybe there was another way. Much as he would love to do it, killing her wouldn't get him anywhere. As it stood now, if Julie died, the house went to that hippie freak; and she hated him as much as he hated her. No, that plan was off the table. The investors were dicking around anyway so maybe, this once, he would be better off to just cut his losses and move on.

Then he remembered that ridiculous story she'd told him about her grandfather and something about hidden valuables. It was probably a huge pile of BS, but he could at least check it out, salvage something for his time. A house that old usually had something worth money in it. If there was something valuable, he had as good a chance as anyone of finding it. After all, he was smarter than everybody he knew.

Now, what had she said again? Something about a magic garden. Well, he wasn't about to go digging up the place; no way to do that without leaving a lot of evidence, and the twit had said some family member had already done that anyway. Stupid to bury valuables, even on your own property; no control, you never knew what could happen.

The best thing to do was to try and think like a crazy old man; see if he could come up with some idea of where else to look. Now, Logan might have a twisted sense of right and wrong, but he was logical and methodical. No matter what the old man said about magic gardens, it made sense to keep his valuables close, either in his rooms or in his office. You wouldn't want just anybody to find your stash; so it had to be someplace obscure. He wouldn't be the kind to stick money in a mattress and take the chance that his legacy would be accidentally sold or given away. No, anybody smart enough to make that kind of dough would not be dumb enough to take a chance on losing it so easily.

That boy, Julius thought, may be a criminal but he has a darned fine mind.

Logan continued to speculate. It depends on what you are hiding, also. He thought about the words Julie used to describe her great-grandfather: **eccentric, inventor**. Guy like that, he'd probably had some family money, to begin with; a family with cash usually has other valuables: probably antiques, jewelry, or art, maybe some gold or silver.

I have to get back in that house and look around, he thought. **If there's anything there, I'll know it. Not tonight, though. She never leaves the house at night. It will have to be during the day.**

Now that he had a plan and no one was actively trying to stop him, Logan was totally calm.

Julius had heard enough for now. Julie was safe for the night, and he had some plans to make of his own.

"**And...**" Gustavia exclaimed when Amethyst did not begin to speak right away.

"I'm not sure if it means anything, but there were a few hot spots in the library: both chairs, near the shelves, and an intensely bright one on the underside of the desk. It could be totally unrelated. It could be from another one of Julie's relatives. It wasn't from her grandmother, though, because I saw her aura mingled with Kat's and it was different."

"Do you think there might be a hidden compartment or something?" Tyler looked at Julie.

"I have no idea; I guess we could take a look," and off they went back up the stairs.

Ammie indicated the area where she could see the aura; and they poked around then searched every inch of the desk for hidden springs, buttons or switches. Tyler removed the drawers and looked behind them to see if there was space enough for a compartment of some kind but found nothing.

Gustavia commented, "Maybe he picked his nose and wiped his boogers under there; my uncle used to do that to his chair. Drove my aunt out of her mind."

There was a chorus of groans, and then they all had a good laugh over the idea. It helped settle the disappointment at not finding anything. Ammie did another pass and saw only a glimmer near one of the bookcases, but nothing large enough to warrant investigation.

By now, it was getting late, and everyone had had enough. It was decided that Julie and Gustavia would bunk in her grandmother's room and the other two girls would take Julie's room. Tyler announced he, too, would be staying and wanted to sleep in Julius' bed. He made a joke about being the only one to sleep alone, so Julie went to her studio and hauled out a large stuffed rabbit that had been a prop in one of her photographs, gave it to him, and—for the third time in an hour—they all trooped back upstairs.

Estelle watched the group as they joked and laughed their way through getting ready for bed. She was happy to see the house filled with the voices of young people again. And when Julius blinked in beside her, she shushed him until everyone was settled.

Back on the gazebo roof, the two had a quick conversation to catch each other up on the night's events. Then Julius decided to check out his bedroom. He wasn't sure he liked the idea of Tyler being in there. It wasn't that he didn't trust him, it was just he still felt a bit nostalgic about his things.

Tyler wasn't asleep; he sat in the bed with his grandfather's notes. There was something about these rooms in those notes. He was sure of it. It was important, or at least he had the niggling feeling that it was, so he was searching through the notes instead of sleeping. As Julius entered the room, Tyler felt a slight chill, more like a stirring of the air than anything. He looked up to see Julius sitting in the chair across from the bed. Now the chill turned to goosebumps. This was unexpected, but he recognized the man from the painting downstairs.

"Good evening, sir. I hope you don't mind me sleeping in your bed," he said.

Now it was Julius' turn to look surprised. He had not meant to appear to the young man and certainly had not expected Tyler to see him without his intention for it to happen.

"Quite alright," he answered thinking to himself that it was no such thing.

"Would you mind if I asked you a few questions?"

"Go ahead, young man; I will answer what I can."

"This was your bedroom. Is there anything here that is out of place, or is it just the way it was when you passed?"

"Nothing different at all; it looks exactly the same. It was a cold, damp winter that year; and unless they kept the fire going day and night, I was always taking a chill."

"Can you tell me anything about the hidden items?"

"Nothing. But what I can tell you is I paid that odious young man a visit."

"Logan?"

"Yes."

"By the way, sir--nice move earlier; I wanted to punch him myself."

Then Julius told Tyler as much as he could about Logan's state of mind but was unable to warn him that the man was planning to sneak back into the house. It was frustrating to know so much and be able to say so little.

Julie and Gustavia settled into the big bed in Estelle's room; neither one thought they would sleep a wink even though it had been a long day.

Gustavia asked, "Jules are you okay? I mean, about Logan?"

"Yes, actually, I am. More okay than I expected to be. He totally had me fooled. I'm still waiting for the **I told you so**.

"Well, you can wait all you want, but you're not getting it. Yeah, he is a complete moron, but that isn't your fault; and neither is the way things turned out. He must have studied you so he would know just what to say and do. You couldn't have known."

"You did."

"Yes, but I didn't like him on principle. He didn't like me, and that meant his judgment had to be completely flawed."

Julie chuckled. "You know what, you're right."

"But, seriously, none of this is in your comfort zip code."

"Zone."

"Whatever. Don't dance around the point. Are you scared? How do you feel?"

"I could never be scared of Grams. Of course, all of this is a little overwhelming, but she came to me earlier and told me to throw caution to the wind. I'm trying to."

"Hmm, Tyler would be helpful in that capacity." Gustavia waggled her eyebrows.

"It's a bit too soon for that kind of thing. I only just met him a few days ago. Funny, though, it seems like I have known him forever. Probably because the last few days have been-- what's the term--**cray cray**?"

"Totally."

"He does have a nice butt, though."
Gustavia snorted at this unexpected
pronouncement.

"Yes, he does; but don't tell him that
or it will go to his head."

"There's a joke in there somewhere,
but I am just too tired to think of it."

And the two women fell asleep
without indulging Tyler's pillow fight
fantasy.

In Julie's room, Amethyst and Kat
settled into twin beds. Ammie was
slightly concerned for her friend
because she had seen overtones of fear
in Kat's aura during the evening. That

was to be expected; but she had also seen a burst of elation.

"Well, that was an unexpected experience."

"Um." Kat's noncommittal response was not going to deter Ammie one bit.

"So, you can just tell me, or we can do the dance, and then you'll tell me anyway. What just happened?"

There was a pause.

"Whenever I channel Julie's grandmother, I can see."

Another pause while Ammie digested that piece of news. Being extremely intuitive, she knew this experience had to be creating mixed emotions. Elation and fear sounded just about right. Then Kat told her story.

"So, even though it developed as a coping mechanism, you are blaming yourself for your blindness, yet feeling thrilled because you know there might be a way to cure it."

"Yeah, Miss Insight; and don't forget angry that I have spent years in the darkness feeling helpless because I have no idea what to do about it."

Ammie's heart flooded with empathy, but she was not about to let Kat wallow.

"Okay, well, I have an idea about that if you are up to hearing it."

Kat shrugged.

"I guess so."

"Has this happened before when you've channeled spirits?"

"No, because I've never actually channeled any spirits like this before. They usually just appear in my mind sort of the way a memory does: kind of fuzzy; and sometimes with sounds, smells; or just a jumble of symbols. If I had a similar experience to theirs, they use my own memories to communicate. Until now, none of them ever actually used my body that way."

"Well, now I get the scary part. That would wig me out, too."

"She was apologetic about it and so gentle, and I could feel how much she cared. And Ammie, she knows. About me seeing and all."

"Then she would probably be willing to help if she could."

"Oh, yes. She is already planning something, she told me tonight. She said, **I know you are the one who usually gives the messages but this time Julie has one for you, ask he**r, but it didn't seem like the right time."

"Why didn't she just give you the message herself if she could talk to you like that?"

"No idea."

She'd heard the message herself; but since Estelle seemed to want it to come from Julie, she'd leave it alone. "We'll find time tomorrow to take her aside so she can tell you. My idea was to ask Estelle for help; but since she's already on it, then I will just offer you my help and support whenever you might need me."

Kat took a deep breath that ended on a sigh, and Amethyst could see much of the tension leaving her body, and her aura was clearing.

"That helps, talking about it helps."

"Anytime."

Chapter Eighteen

Thinking he was the first one out of bed the next morning, Tyler quietly navigated the stairs with a single thought in mind: coffee. He needed a vat of coffee. After his visit with Julius, sleep had not come easy. Now, his brain felt fuzzy, the kind of fuzzy that required caffeine. Lots and lots of caffeine.

Before he got to the kitchen, he knew someone else had beaten him to the punch. He could smell it: coffee and something else. Bacon and eggs? This must be heaven.

Kat was buttering a pile of toast while Gustavia, decked out in a frilly 1950's-style apron, manned the stove. Julie was setting the table, and Amethyst had the beverages covered. Along with the coffee, she had brewed a pot of tea. One look at Tyler had her grabbing the coffee pot and pouring him a cup. He sank into a chair and gulped about half a cup of the hot nectar without even blinking. Moments later the fog began to clear, and he looked up to see three pairs of amused eyes looking back at him, and Kat with a smirk on her face that told him she hadn't needed to see him to figure out what state he was in.

Turning back to the stove, Gustavia proved she could have gotten a job anywhere as a short-order cook serving up perfectly cooked sunny-side-up and scrambled eggs, hash browns, and veggie bacon. That last earned a skeptical look from Tyler, but when in Rome--and it turned out to be not half bad. They packed away the food while making light conversation, then loaded up the dishwasher and settled into the living room to compare thoughts from their previous night's experience. He described his talk with Julius, then began to lay out a series of observations he had been pondering.

His findings were eerily similar to Logan's musings from the night before, but he was blissfully unaware of that fact.

"Julius was an unconventional thinker, but it takes logic to invent useful things. If we follow the logic, then it seems like he probably wouldn't have hidden valuables outside. It's much more likely he would have wanted anything that important nearby, where he could keep watch over it.

"Okay, that all makes sense, but then how does the magic garden figure into the equation?" Julie still had the annoying sensation she'd seen the phrase somewhere before this all happened, but she still couldn't quite pull the memory to the front of her mind. Frustrating.

"I'm not sure. They told you not to think literally; that probably means there is no actual garden to dig up, so there is probably nothing buried on the grounds. The first thing that springs to mind when I hear the word **literally** is a book, but that's not what they said."

"I tore the library apart looking for that family history. I am sure, if there were a book with that title, I would have noticed it; so you're probably right."

"Okay," he added the information to his computerized notes. "My grandfather researched the house quite thoroughly when he was compiling the family history, and there were no references to any hidden passageways, which was another thought I had. If we figure Julius was logical and wanted to keep his valuables both safe and in a location he could monitor, a hidden room would be ideal. Julie, do you have any records of work done to the house? Maybe he had something built on the sly."

"Not offhand, but there are boxes of papers in the attic; there might be something in one of them."

Amethyst chimed in. "A tree fell on my uncle's house once; and when the workmen came to do the repairs, he had them put in the skylight he had always wanted. He said it was the perfect time to do it since half the roof had to come off anyway. It's possible something was added at the same time something else was repaired, so watch for those types of records also."

"I am not sure about repairs, but I know at least some of the bathrooms were modernized, and there was extensive electrical work done. It was a long time ago, and some of it needs to be updated again." Julie sighed.

"He wouldn't have hidden anything valuable in an object that might be sold, broken, or lost. I could tell that about him within two minutes of talking to him. So, if my theories are correct, whatever it is we are looking for must be somewhere in the house."

Gustavia pouted. "No more dowsing, and I was just getting good at it."

Kat had been silent through the entire conversation, but now she spoke up.

"I think you're right, Tyler. I got a pretty good idea of his personality when he was talking through me. Too bad I couldn't see into his mind more, I might have been able to lead you right to the hiding place. But, my intuition tells me we are on the right track."

A thought struck Tyler.

"Do you get impressions when you handle objects?"

"Sometimes, but not the way I think you mean. I can't pick up a pen and see what documents he signed with it, or hold his cuff links and see what he did while wearing them."

"Okay, moving on. Following this train of thought to its logical conclusion, we should think about what exactly it is that we are looking for; if we know the items, it will be easier to figure out what spaces they would fit into best. Papers would be easier to hide and harder to find. I know there are records of family silver and jewelry. Jewelry would fit in a smallish place, but silver is going to take up some room. Do we think his workshop is a possibility? He did have it built from scratch so he could have added a hidden space."

Julie thought for a minute. "Maybe. We can check; but, as far as I know, Grams went through the whole place when she turned it into a museum. Unless there is some sort of false bottom or back area in his cabinets, I think it would be another waste of time."

"Then we concentrate on the house first and keep the workshop as a last resort. Julie says there was a reference to some silver and jewelry that have never turned up; so, unless he sold them for capital, those should still be here somewhere. But that doesn't account for his own money. Could his inventions have eaten up an entire fortune? Or did he invest the money in something else? Stocks, bonds, precious metals or more jewels?"

"Not jewels; great-grandfather had little use for them; he called them **glitters**. Grams used to laugh about it. She said he thought the only value of diamonds was to use them for cutting and grinding, and why did women want to go around wearing shiny rocks anyway. When she said gold and silver were shiny, too, he couldn't contradict her, so he blustered about it for weeks."

"Stocks and bonds are registered and would have shown up during probate if he had a will. I have clients who book readings thinking they can untangle probate problems by talking to dead relatives. Never works," Kat said.

"Yes, that's right. Did he have a will?" Gustavia asked.

"He must have; there should be a copy of it in those records in the attic."

Amethyst looked at her watch. "This is a great start, but I have to be getting home; I have a couple of readings scheduled this afternoon."

"Me, too," Kat agreed.

Tyler volunteered himself for taxi duty thinking he would stop at home and pack a bag. After his talk with Julius, he knew Julie should not be alone in the house until things were resolved. It was no hardship to stand guard duty. He could work from anywhere. He and Gustavia had that in common, so it made sense for them to be the ones who took turns staying at Hayward House.

Gustavia stayed behind to help straighten up, she said. Julie knew better; she knew she was being managed, that they had made a plan not to leave her alone. Funny how a person could be both annoyed and thankful at the same time.

By unspoken agreement, they avoided the subjects of treasure, ghosts, Logan, and even Tyler. Gustavia talked about the book she was currently writing. This one was about a dragon who had lost his mother; it was inspired by a little girl she'd met at a library reading. She quoted some sections that Julie found enchanting. Her friend had a way with words.

Turning her attention to her own work, Julie booted up the computer in her studio and ran a slide show of her mirror series. They were good, but there was something missing. The two tossed around some ideas then, as Gustavia leaned over to take a closer look at the setup, she put her head in just the right position for her reflected face to appear in each of the mirrored panels.

"Hold it right there." Julie flipped on the lighting, then grabbed her camera, and quickly began shooting. "Okay, turn your head just a bit to the right." The shutter fired in rapid sequence as she moved around the perimeter of the scene. "Give me just a bit more neck-- that's it--tilt your head back a bit more." Gustavia was used to these types of instructions; she had posed for Julie many times before.

It took only a matter of minutes before Julie put down the camera. "Done. Want to see what we have?" She transferred the images, then fired up Photoshop as Gustavia pulled up a second chair to watch. Julie moved the images into a new folder naming it with the date and subject matter. She tried to keep things as organized as possible.

Following a well-established workflow, she zoomed in to look for and remove any unwanted specks, stray hairs or dust; cropped the photo to center the one reflection she thought should be the focal point; then added a curves layer, tweaking the image, one color at a time, to add a bit more drama. It was coming together nicely. She would take the time later to give this the attention it deserved; but, for now, she was just playing with some ideas.

Gustavia watched as the area around the central image of her face was softened and blurred, so it looked as though her features were appearing out of a fog. She could see where Julie was headed with this idea, and it was going to be good.

Tyler found them there, so totally absorbed in the creation of art neither had heard him come in. He wasn't trying to scare them, but when he looked over their shoulders, he couldn't help but say, "Wow!" Both women jumped, then turned on him. He barely noticed, he was riveted to the screen. Thttps://wfa.kronostm.com/index.jsp?applicationName=NewCastleHotelsNonReqExt&locale=en_UShen he looked up at the framed images that marched down the wall.

"You. You're J.L. Hayward."

He turned his attention to Gustavia, tilting his head first left, then right. "And, you're the lady in the blue series, aren't you?"

They both nodded in amusement. "I have three of your prints hanging above my bed. Small world."

Chapter Nineteen

Tamara's images were finished, and Julie just needed to drive into town and drop off the files. It would have been easier to email them, but she still wanted to get a look at that map. Of course, Tyler offered to tag along. He said it was because he wanted to stop at the grocery store, but Julie knew better.

Smiling to herself, Gustavia watched the tension start to set in and wondered if Julie even realized half of what she was feeling was due to the attraction building between the two of them. Well, she would do her part and make herself scarce so they could get on with it. Or, get it on. Was it wicked to hope they did?

On her way out, just for the fun of it, she hugged each of them and, as she did, she whispered in Tyler's ear, "Go get her, champ," then laughed, as his face froze in consternation. Still chuckling, she made her way out the door. This was going to be a much better match. They were made for each other. Her turn for finding love had better be coming, though, and soon.

As she walked through her front door, Gustavia heard the text alert on her phone. Zack. A short text; just three words--**Be there tomorrow**. Oh, great. Just what she needed. But, for Julie's sake, she would put up with a lot, even her brother. Her return text was even shorter--**Okay**.

Oakville was a small town located just close enough to the city to take advantage of its conveniences, but far enough away to avoid high crime rates. Being situated on the edge of the lake brought just enough tourism to keep the eclectic mix of main street shops in business all year round.

Of course, living in a small town also came with both the advantage and disadvantage of everyone knowing everyone else, so Julie knew tongues would start wagging when she showed up with Tyler in tow instead of Logan. Still, she might as well face the gossip head-on; her engagement was over, and if she didn't tell her story, people would make up their own. Admittedly, the stories that spread were often wildly exaggerated; but, in this case, she was pretty sure the truth was stranger than any possible fiction.

"You know we'll both be the subject of intense gossip and scrutiny, right?" Since Tyler hadn't grown up here, Julie figured it was a good idea to warn him about what he was getting himself into.

"Why, what did I do?" He was puzzled.

"It's not what you've done but what they think you've done. Everyone in town knows I was engaged; and when I show up ringless and with another man, they'll all assume you broke us up."

"Ah, a Lothario. So that makes you, what, a hapless female unable to resist my many wiles?"

"Or a Jezebel with no sense of loyalty or honor. Too fickle to commit to one man."

"Are you sure it will be that bad? I don't want to cause you any trouble."

"No, don't worry; people know I'm not the Jezebel type. But you? You they don't know; so I'm afraid Lothario it is."

His wicked grin showed he relished the idea.

"It's been such a mad time that I don't think you've had the chance to tell me if you moved here or are just visiting."

"My work carried me all over the world; it's been amazing except for the living out of suitcases part. A month or so ago, I was talking to my grandfather on the phone and realized something was off. As soon as I filed that story, I took a leave of absence and came here."

"How's he doing?"

"He's getting better; it turned out to be a side effect of one of his medications. He realized something was wrong but was having a hard time communicating it to his doctors. It was pretty scary, but he's doing a bit better every day."

"That's great news."

"I'm thankful I didn't go the nine-to-five route, or I wouldn't have had the flexibility to be here when he needed me."

"So, you'll be leaving soon, then." She was surprised by how disappointed she felt at the prospect of his going away soon.

"My plans are up in the air right now. It seems I don't miss the globe-trotting life as much as I expected. It's been nice to stay in one place for more than a week, getting to know new people, and especially spending time with my grandfather. I've been helping him finish a project he'd been hired to do for a historical website, and the work is fascinating. And, just lately I've found the town has some other fascinating attractions."

Julie pulled into a small parking lot behind the gallery. "Here we go,

Lothario. You sure you're ready for this?"

"Lead on."

As they entered her shop, Tamara pulled off the thick magnifying glasses she used for close work. She wasn't a vain woman, but those things were a look even a supermodel couldn't pull off—sort of half dork, half alien. Greeting Julie warmly, she then turned her attention to Tyler giving him the once-over and making him blush.

"So, this is new." Her tone was speculative but approving.

"This is Tyler Kingsley, Barrett's grandson. He's been helping me with research on the house."

"I'll just bet he has." She all but hummed the words.

Now it was Julie's turn to blush.

"Tamara, it isn't like that."

"You mean you haven't tossed out the city boy yet?"

"No, he's gone."

Tamara let out a whoop. "It's about time. Goodbye Mr. Pompous. Came in here once, looked around with a condescending smirk on his face, and walked out without a word. I knew right then he was the wrong one for you. Too snobby, if you ask me."

She raised an eyebrow at the grin her opinion put on Tyler's face and figured Julie may think it **wasn't like that,** but he was definitely interested.

Setting the record straight, Tyler said, "Not just a snob, but a con man and dangerous, to boot. He has no reason to come back to town; but if you do see him around, it would help if you could call one of us." He wrote down his cell phone number and passed it along to Tamara.

"Count on it," she said ignoring Julie's exasperated sigh and the exaggerated shake of her head. "Want me to pass the word? He hasn't made many friends in town."

"Sure." He was still grinning and also ignoring Julie as her gestures of protest became more emphatic.

Tamara, eyes twinkling moved behind the counter to pull out the copy of the map she had made and pass it across to Julie.

"I hope this helps. All joking aside, if he truly is dangerous, I don't like the idea of you being in that big old house alone."

"Well, that's not a problem since this one here and Gustavia have taken it upon themselves to provide rotating guard duty whether I want it or not." Julie feigned exasperation until she saw Tamara's knowing smile and then her annoyance turned real in spite of her gratitude toward her friends.

Thanking Tamara and promising to keep her posted, they left the shop. Julie wanted to stomp away in a huff over his inclination to overshare her personal business with someone he had just met, but knowing Tyler's motivations were pure made the act seem childish,   so she contented herself with a narrow-eyed glare and crossed arms. Her stance did nothing whatsoever to put a dent in his good humor, so she was unable to maintain any level of annoyance. What was she going to do with him? The devil on her shoulder whispered a few choice answers to that question, and her face flamed red. Tyler's eyes widened in question, but Julie just shook her head and walked across the street to the grocery store.

She held her silence for about two minutes. "You realize she is the worst gossip in town; and by the time we get to the checkout, the grapevine will be humming, right? Look, over there," she bobbed her head to the side to indicate a woman busily texting, "That's Emily Snowden, Tamara's next-door-neighbor; and I'd put money on us being the subject of that text."

Sure enough, Emily hit the send key and, looking up, caught sight of Julie. With the guilty look of someone caught in the act, she grasped her cart and scurried down the next aisle. Waiting a few seconds then gesturing for him to follow her, Julie spun right and then left, and there was Emily, busily typing in another text. She grabbed Tyler by the arm and backed silently around the corner then strode down the next aisle over and looped back for a full frontal assault on Emily and her cart.

"Hello, Emily; how's it going?"

"Fine." Shame written all over her face, she tried to bluff it out. "And how are you?"

"I feel fantastic. Make sure you say hi to Tamara for me, okay? See you later."

She turned to Tyler.

"What should we have for dinner? I'm in the mood for chicken." She turned and made her way purposefully toward the meat counter. Glancing over his shoulder, Tyler saw Emily furiously thumbing away at her next text and snorted.

With each passing day, it became clearer to him that Logan had not had a clue what kind of woman he was dealing with. This was not a woman who needed or wanted a man to handle the details. She may not be as flamboyant as Gustavia, but she didn't shrink from a confrontation, and she also didn't feel the need to belittle anyone. She'd clearly made her point to Emily, the texting gossip; but without meanness or prevarication. It didn't hurt that she was sexy when she was mad, either. He realized he was already falling for her, but he didn't see any reason to try and stop himself. Getting her to fall for him, well, that might take some doing, but he was up for the challenge.

Julie made her way through the store, greeting each person she met by name, but not stopping to make conversation. As predicted, when they got to the checkout, the cashier, Amanda, according to her name tag, glanced pointedly at Julie's left hand noting the absence of an engagement ring, offered a sympathetic smile, then gave a speculative look at Tyler, which did nothing to lighten the mood. He followed her out to the car and helped her transfer the groceries into the back seat. She got points for not slamming the door before she slid behind the wheel.

"Well, wasn't that just a thrilling experience?" Julie twisted the key to start the engine.

Tyler chuckled. Julie glowered. Tyler laughed harder. The corners of her mouth began to twitch. Just a little at first and then a little more until, finally, they were both laughing too hard to breathe.

"Did you see the look on Emily's face when she saw me standing there?"

"Caught her red-handed. Or would that be red thumbed since she was texting?"

"It isn't funny."

"One thing you can count on, you set the tone for what people will be saying about you. No one is going to say you're moping around broken-hearted over the ending of your engagement."

"Once Tamara passes the word about Logan, he'll find it hard to sneak back into the area without someone seeing him. You're okay with most of the town having your cell phone number within the hour, right?"

"If it keeps you safer, that's fine with me."

"I know. It's hard to stay mad at people for gossiping when you know they have your back. It's frustrating when everyone knows your business; but, at the same time, it's also comforting to know they care. Small towns can be a lot like a family, I suppose."

It hadn't seemed like a big deal to have Tyler stay the night until it was actually happening. Now Julie was surprised to find herself feeling just a little bit nervous. She'd only known him for a matter of days; and even if he fit into her ever-widening circle of friends like he'd always been there, it was still weird how he felt the need to protect her. Even weirder that she didn't mind all that much.

For the second time, Julie and Tyler prepared a meal in her kitchen, moving around each other as though they'd had years of practice. Her tension quickly melted under his warmth and humor. It amazed her how comfortable she felt with him. Not well-worn-shoe comfortable but warm-fuzzy-blanket comfortable. It was nice.

"Should I sleep in Julius' room again?" Tyler asked.

"Um, sure, if you're comfortable there. Or, you could use one of the other bedrooms. You never know, he might decide to visit you again."

"Listen, I don't mind admitting that it was a strange experience. Interesting, but strange. I don't think it much matters which room I'm sleeping in; if he wants to talk, he'll just show up."

"Tell me about it. My life has become a series of strange experiences lately, and it's a bit overwhelming. I mean, here you are, basically a stranger, sleeping over in my great-grandfather's bed."

Dramatically, Tyler clutched his heart as though mortally wounded. "A stranger, she says. Well, I feel like I've known you forever."

"That's just because this week has felt like an eternity. Do you really think Logan would dare to show up here?" She changed the subject before she was tempted to tell him it felt like forever to her, too.

"Your grandfather does, and that's good enough for me. I don't trust the guy and not just because I know he's a crook. He was going to hit you yesterday, and he wanted to hit you the other day, too." Tyler's eyes sparked with indignation. Hitting a woman was right down there with the lowest of the low things a man could do.

"I know." She shook her head. It was difficult to comprehend that Logan had not been the man she'd thought he was; that he would even contemplate violence just proved how far off her perceptions of him had been.

Reaching across the table, Tyler laid a warm hand on hers. It was a simple gesture, one of friendly support, but the jolt it sent through her system didn't feel friendly at all. No, it felt red hot and charged with intention. Julie gazed across the table. Tyler gazed back; both lost in the connection of hearts and souls recognizing each other. Hand still tingling, Julie felt as though the universe took a breath then settled into a new rhythm: one that had her heart beating, fluttering against her throat as she saw the mirror of her feelings in Tyler's eyes. Her hand began to tremble as, without letting it go, Tyler stood, then walked around the table, gently drew her to her feet and, still gazing into her eyes, lowered his lips to hers.

The tingle she'd felt when their hands connected was nothing compared to the shock of lips meeting lips. Julie pulled back for a moment; then, sighing, poured herself totally into a kiss that set Tyler's knees shaking. She hadn't expected this. Fire ran through her veins; molten streams heated her skin and left her breathless.

The taste of her, the texture of her lips filled him until he could think of nothing else, just this experience, this one moment. If it lasted a lifetime, it would never be enough.

He cupped her face tenderly in his hand, caressing her cheek with his thumb then moved his lips up to gently kiss each eyelid as she breathed out on a sigh. Julie's hands slid into his hair, teasing through the silky strands until she whispered **more** and pulled his mouth back to hers in a second scorching kiss. He gathered her closer and closer until he could feel the thunder of her heart against his own. Finally, though it was the last thing he wanted to do, Tyler gently pulled back and rested his forehead against hers.

"If we keep that up, Julius will be visiting me in your room, and it's too soon."

"Oh, I think I could be persuaded." Julie was surprised by how easy it would be. He'd undone her with a kiss; and she wanted to see what else he could do to her, what she could do to him. "Why is it too soon?" Then Julie leaned back and looked at his face. He was blushing; she quirked an eyebrow. Something else was going on here. She might not have known Tyler long, but she darn sure knew he wasn't easily embarrassed. Then it dawned on her.

"Oh my God! You think Julius or Grams might be around, and you don't want to do it in front of a ghost." The idea of it made her laugh. Realizing he might just have a point only made it worse. Trying to maintain an air of injured dignity and failing miserably, Tyler waited until she got hold of herself.

"I can see why you find this amusing..." he protested, then trailed off as Julie wiping the tears from her eyes held up a hand for him to stop.

"No, it's not you; it's just this whole situation. For the last few days, it's felt like I took a wrong turn into crazy town. Kissing you was the first thing that's felt completely right in longer than I even realized. The idea that we could easily have had sweaty, jungle sex right here on the kitchen table with my dead grandmother watching is just...well..." Julie twirled a finger at her temple.

Without saying a word, Tyler drew her into a warm embrace, resting his chin on her head as she snuggled closer. Both were thinking this felt right, like coming home. It didn't matter that they'd only known each other for a short time; he didn't care if they never found her family heirlooms; as long as she kept him around, he would be happy.

Then he whispered, "Julie. Look."

Turning her head, she saw Grams standing by the door, grinning from ear to ear. Then, she was gone. Julie facepalmed. Tyler grinned. Vindicated.

"Looks like we'll need to set some boundaries if we ever want to be alone. Or find whatever is hidden." Tyler led Julie into the living room and opened his laptop to start going over his notes again.

Chapter Twenty

Zack stood on his sister's front steps, loathe to knock on the door. He looked at the outside of the house trying to get some clue about what he might find on the inside. A carefully tended garden filled the front yard. Artfully arranged to look as though it had just sprung up naturally, it was obvious a lot of care had gone into its planning. Weathered cedar shake siding gave the compactly built home a cottage-like feel. He found it charming, not that he would ever come out and say that to his sister.

He raised a hand, but before he could knock Gustavia swung open the door. "Were you planning to stand on the step all night?" she asked.

"No, I was just getting ready to...never mind. Are you going to let me in?"

Gustavia wasn't sure how she felt about his being there. No one from her biological family had ever visited before. Deep inside, she was sure there was a kernel of happiness that should be sprouting; but, right now, she felt she was being invaded. He was going to leave his vibes of disapproval all over the place; and, when he was gone, she'd have to sage the whole house. **Too bad**, she thought, stepping back to let him in.

"Yeah, I am."

Eager to get this over with, he barely looked at the living room. Gustavia had a knack for blending items of different styles into an eclectic mix that actually worked together. The walls were lined with her own artwork, some of Julie's photos, and a couple of Estelle's paintings. It was a cozy room, warm and welcoming. Not that Zack seemed to notice as he handed her the file he'd amassed on Logan.

"It's bad." Then, he waited, watching her closely while she scanned through the documents.

"Yeah, I can see that. She's not going to be safe until he's caught, is she?" Gustavia looked up at her brother with concern. Zack shook his head. Problem was his gut was telling him Julie wasn't the only one in danger.

"I don't think so. Think he might come after you, too?"

"Kat said there was danger for both of us."

"Kat?"

"She's my friend, the psychic." Zack snorted and rolled his eyes. Gustavia narrowed hers.

"Don't start in on my **lifestyle**," she sneered and made air quotes, "I know you don't approve of me; that's nothing new."

"Let's not get into our twisted family dynamic, and I don't want to hear anything about your psychic friend. You know the man, I don't. What does your instinct tell you? Are you safe?"

"He doesn't like me. In fact, I think he hates me, and I wouldn't put anything past him. But I can take care of myself."

"Oh, what are you going to do if he comes after you? Throw a crystal at him? Chant? Jingle those bells in your hair?"

Gustavia contained her fury, just barely.

"I can take care of myself," she said through gritted teeth resisting the temptation to throw down some Krav Maga on him right then and there. Oh, she'd chant while she kicked his ass, then he'd see whose bells got jingled.

"I think you're probably safe enough until he realizes I'm onto him. Then he's going to do one of two things: he's either going to run or try for revenge."

"He knows there may be something valuable in Hayward House. He'll go for that and for Julie long before he gets any ideas about coming after me. We

413

need to come up with a plan to catch him."

"Does Julie's house have a security system? I can see this one doesn't."

"No, but Tyler's with Julie. Tomorrow night will be my turn; we're alternating nights so she won't be alone."

"That's a start." Gustavia had a few plans of her own for setting up a sort of alarm system: trip wires and booby traps that she wasn't going to tell her brother about. He sneered at her enough as it was.

"Okay then, I guess I'm out of here." Even in this state of perpetual annoyance with his sister, Zack didn't feel right about leaving her alone.

Sensing his reluctance and that he was leaving something unsaid, Gustavia followed her instincts and invited him to dinner then was surprised when he accepted. Was there any safe topic for conversation? Probably not. **Just breathe, let the tension go,** she thought, while making an effort to unclench her jaw. **Give him a chance.**

Maybe after all these years, they could find some kind of common ground, something to talk about that wouldn't devolve into the same old fight. She wasn't living up to the Roman standards, blah, blah, blah. She could do so much more with her life, yada, yada, yada. Whatever. Gustavia was happy with her life, her work, and her friends; why was that never enough for her brother? Giving herself a little mental shake, she let go of the tension that had crept back into her body again.

What in the world was he thinking? This was either going to turn into a fight or an hour or so of awkward silence, the same as always. Zack admitted to himself that he'd always wished things could be different, that he could have a better relationship with Eloise. Even in his thoughts, he refused to use her crazy new name. Taking a deep breath, he finally looked around at the home his sister had made for herself. He was thinking, from what he could see of it, it seemed comfortable and homey. A far cry from the somewhat sterile place they'd grown up in. **Not going to open that can of worms**, he thought. One particular painting drew his eye.

"Who's the artist?" Zack pointed to the watercolor abstract. Bold washes of blue and green tones shot through with a glittering gold line that bisected the canvas diagonally produced a piece with a visceral impact. It made him think of swimming up toward the surface of the ocean.

"That's one of mine."

"Really?"

"Yeah, really. I'm so flattered by your obvious surprise."

Really? Ten minutes in and he'd already screwed up, and this time he wasn't even trying to tick her off.

"I'm sorry, I didn't know you painted. I thought you wrote books for kids."

"Well, I do lots of things, I'm a woman of many talents." Her dry tone of voice helped spread a thin veneer of annoyance over the ache of once again knowing she hadn't measured up, he hadn't believed in her. Not wanting him to see the pain in her eyes, Gustavia concentrated on the sauce she was stirring.

Silence.

Finally, she looked up. Was that an apologetic look on his face? Be easier to tell if she'd ever seen one before. She dropped the mask of anger and let him see the sorrow that had lived in her for so many years.

Quietly he spoke. "I've read your books, all of them. They're good."

Gustavia ducked her head to hide the tears that had welled up at his simple acceptance of at least this one thing about her.

"Really good," he repeated.

She only nodded. The urge to hug him was strong, but she'd been burned in the past by expecting acceptance from the people in her life that should have loved her and didn't seem able to do so. "So is this painting."

"Thank you." Gustavia sighed. **Now what**, she thought. **Say something. No, don't speak, if you do, it will somehow be the wrong words**.

She stirred the sauce then dropped the pasta into the now boiling pot. The silence lengthened to the point of awkwardness. A quick glance told her Zack had turned back to gaze at the painting again, so she did a quick shoulder roll to loosen the tightness that seemed to return every few minutes.

"Are you doing any painting these days?" He shrugged.

"These two over here aren't yours, are they? Zack deflected the conversation away from himself.

"No, Julie's grandmother painted those. They were birthday gifts."

"Are they insured? I know one of her pieces sold well at auction recently. These could be worth money." It was a simple question; and Zack couldn't have predicted the reason it caused such a reaction when Gustavia informed him through clenched teeth that, to her, the paintings were priceless, but not insured. How could he not understand their value lie in the fact that they were gifts given with love? That Gram's love, while it meant the world to Gustavia, couldn't quite make up for the lack of it she'd received from her own family. She set the table with barely controlled fury, placing the plates and utensils none too gently in their places then gestured for him to sit.

Yep, she was mad again. What had he said this time? He went over the conversation in his mind and couldn't see where he'd gone wrong. He'd complimented her—not once, but twice—and asked a perfectly normal question. This was the longest time they'd spent in the same room without shouting at each other. He didn't understand why but his gut, the one he listened to every day on the job, failed him around his sister. It was easy to understand a perp's motivation for stealing, but she just wasn't readable; he had never been able to get a handle on her.

She'd come from a good family, a family of normal people. Sure, maybe they weren't the most demonstrative of people, maybe they had expectations for each other, but they were still decent, upstanding citizens. Why couldn't she just be normal like the rest of them? She could still write her books. All she had to do was buy some decent clothes, go to a hairdresser once in a while, and stop hanging out with those **psychic** nut jobs.

Eyes narrowed, Gustavia watched his face and knew exactly what he was thinking. It wasn't hard to figure out since these were the same themes he trotted out every time they were in a room together for more than ten minutes. For just a fleeting moment, she'd thought he'd changed, that he might just have begun to understand her a little; but, no.

It was futile to keep expecting things to ever be different between them, so Zack turned the subject back to Logan; the rest of the meal was spent speculating what he might do next. An hour later, Zack was out the door congratulating himself; they'd spent more than an hour together, and there'd been no shouting.

Meanwhile, Gustavia was washing dishes and thinking nothing had changed. She would have been shocked if she'd known Zack had driven around the block and then parked his car a few hundred feet from her driveway. She would have been royally miffed if she'd known he'd flattened a clump of daffodils while navigating the perimeter of her property to see if Logan could find an easy way in. She would have been stunned if she'd known he settled into his car for the night to keep watch over her. They might fight like cats and dogs, but no one was going to mess with his sister.

No one.

Chapter Twenty-One

"How do you make sense of this?" Julie asked Tyler as she frowned at his computer screen.

"It's a mind map, which is just a different name for a flow chart. It helps me see connections between the information more dimensionally than a simple list.

"Geek." Julie smiled. He just smirked.

"I have lists, too," he pulled up several more pages, "a timeline, and I scanned my grandfather's notes, so everything is here. It felt like we were getting somewhere earlier with the ideas about where the most sensible hiding places might be. Leaving the magic garden thing out of it, the library or Julius' suite seems logical. If we had a better idea of what we were looking for it would help, but I think we are beginning to narrow it down."

"Then there's the key. All the keys I have fit locks somewhere in the house; there are none I can't account for. I've barely given it any thought since I figured we needed to find that magic garden before we knew what kind of key to look for."

"Sensible, as always," Tyler smiled.

"Right." Julie thought for a moment. "The clues we have are pretty cryptic."

"True. So, if **the magic garden will bring the light** and you are not supposed to think literally, the question is what are we missing? Whose words provide the most information?" Tyler's fingers flew over the keyboard as he opened a new document. "Since he is the one who did the hiding, let's start with your grandfather; can you remember exactly what he said to you?"

Julie made a face. "Most of it, I guess. I was kind of freaked out that first time. **It all starts with the magic garden** was the gist of it. He kept repeating that. Then the second time he told me not to sign Logan's papers, and that's about it. Oh, and there's the story of his last words about the garden, the key, and possibility he was gesturing to his left." She paused a moment to picture the room in her mind. "The way his bedroom is laid out, he would have been pointing toward the empty wall; doesn't make sense. Oh, and Grams also said we don't have much time before this cycle ends, whatever that means."

Tyler recorded these statements then added his conversation with Julius from the night before. It was not much to go on, next to nothing really. Still, there had to be something they were missing. Julie's words triggered that feeling he was missing something obvious, but what?

"**The magic garden brings the ligh**t, that's an odd turn of phrase. Gardens don't generally bring light, but they do need it. He didn't tell you to start **in** the magic garden but to start **with** it. That means there must be a magic garden that exists right now. **Don't think literally** probably means there is no book called the **Magic**

Garden in the library, or that the garden isn't the kind planted in the dirt."

"I thought there might be, but when I looked for the family history, I didn't notice any books by that title. The only thing I found was a copy of **The Secret Garden**. But I still have the feeling I've seen those words written somewhere."

As she was talking, Tyler Googled the phrase, just in case, and found that Gene Straiten-Porter had written a book called the **Magic Garden**. It had been published in 1927, which fit perfectly into his timeline. He showed Julie a picture of the plain green cover with the title inside a decorative frame, both in gold. "Maybe this will jog your memory. Do you remember ever seeing this book?"

"I'm not sure. A lot of old books have plain covers like that."

"We may be getting closer, but it doesn't feel that way. I keep circling back to my conversation with your grandfather. He said something I thought was important at the time, but it was such a surreal experience—and by the time it was over, the thought was gone—and now I just can't seem to pull it back into focus."

Julie nodded, "I know, I've been feeling the same way. It's so frustrating." Tyler patted her knee then saved his work and closed the laptop.

"Look, let's take a break from all this, watch a movie or something, let our subconscious work on it for a while."

Julie made popcorn while Tyler browsed her DVD collection. She returned to find him slack-jawed in front of the open cabinet.

"There's nothing here, but chick flicks, musicals and documentaries."

"Guess you'll have to deal with it," Julie shrugged, "I have a thing for 80's movies. **Sixteen Candles**, **Breakfast Club**, **The Goonies**, **Say Anything**. C'mon, you have to admit the boom box scene is iconic." Tyler quirked an eyebrow and shrugged.

"You've never seen it?" When he shrugged again to indicate no, it was decided. They settled on the couch with the popcorn between them, but each hyper-aware of the other.

Tyler was amazed to watch out of the corner of his eyes as Julie mouthed each line along with the actors. Clearly, she had seen this movie many times before; he found it charming. However, within a few short minutes, he became absorbed in the story. By the time Lloyd Dobler, with his sleeves pushed up, coat billowing, held up his boom box to serenade the girl of his dreams, Tyler was rooting for him. Using her peripheral vision, Julie watched him as he got into it; he couldn't help himself.

She needed this break from the craziness that had become her life. Had it only been a week or so? It felt like longer. Taking stock of the changes, she thought that, on balance, they were mostly for the good. She'd made some new friends and come to accept their unique abilities. Pretty hard to discount aura readings when you were being visited by dead relatives on an almost daily basis.

Ammie might not look **normal**, but she was a sweet person who beat a mean drum. Julie figured it wasn't likely she'd be scheduling weekly tarot card readings, but spending time with Kat didn't scare her anymore. The psychic had a great sense of humor, and her description of how she came to sense spirits showed she was more grounded and down-to-earth than she seemed. That made Julie a lot more comfortable.

There was a possibility, even if it was slim, that they would find something valuable enough to pay for fixing up her house without having to subdivide and sell off bits of the property. Finding out Logan was a criminal who was trying to con her was still a bit hard to swallow, though.

On the one hand, she was glad she'd found out now before he'd been able to follow through with his plan; but, on the other, she was annoyed she hadn't seen through him sooner. Julie had always considered herself to be a good judge of character. In that context, her relationship had been an epic fail. Why hadn't she seen it, and why didn't she feel more upset over the breakup? Sure, meeting Tyler may have had something to do with her response; but, to be brutally honest, what she actually felt was relief and a weird sense of detachment as though the whole thing had happened to someone else.

Sitting on this couch watching a movie and holding Tyler's hand felt more real, more comfortable, yet more exciting than any moment she'd ever spent with Logan; that was something to think about. Later. Right now, she'd rather think about Tyler, those toe-curling kisses, the strength of the long fingers firmly clasping her own, the feel of his thumb as it caressed the back of her hand sending tingles through her body. Yeah, next time Grams showed up, they were going to have a talk about setting some boundaries.

Estelle, in her customary perch on the gazebo roof, was elated. Her girl had finally found the one, and he was just perfect. Julius shimmered in beside her.

"What are you so happy about?"

"Julie and Tyler kissed," Julius grunted his indifference. He'd been hanging around here long enough; he wanted to get this mess sorted out so he could move on. Whatever else happened, his granddaughter was now in control of his own afterlife, and it grated. He also knew she was trying her best, but he was getting anxious. If they missed this cycle, it would be another year before they could try again.

"Any news on the search? Are they moving forward at all? There's less than a month before she has to use the key."

"How should I know? Since you can't or won't tell me what they're looking for or where to find it, I don't have a clue if they are getting any closer. I told her **the magic garden will bring the light**; and I don't even know what that means, just that I was supposed to say it. They've decided to concentrate on the library and your rooms, but that's all I know."

At that, Julius smiled. "They're on the right track. I gave that young man a vital clue, but he didn't quite catch it. All they need to do now is put their heads together, and they'll figure it out. What's more important at the moment is that we need to sort out some kind of plan. That Logan intends to break into the house. He's decided to believe there's something to find and has already narrowed his focus down to those same areas. He's got a devious mind; too bad he uses it to hurt instead of help."

"Can you teach me that trick you used on him before? Or at least show me how to put up a barrier. Between us, we should be able to keep him from getting inside."

That was only a last resort, he explained. It took a little energy to show yourself to someone with sensitivity enough to see; it took a lot of energy to affect the physical world strongly enough to create a barrier and hold it for any length of time. He figured, between the two of them, they could delay the inevitable by only a few minutes before their energy ran out. That would leave the house vulnerable for as long as it took to recharge. Not an ideal situation. Guys like Logan didn't deter easily once they had a plan. So if they were going to stop him, it was time to up the ante. Julius knew he just needed to figure out how.

Throwing the covers off her heated body, Julie tossed and turned trying to get comfortable. Overwhelmed by the events of the past few days, she couldn't seem to settle; and knowing

Tyler was just down the hall didn't help one bit. The man had gotten under her skin, and it also didn't help that he kissed like the devil; which was unexpected since he came across as a nice, low-key, sort of nerdy type of guy, the kind that wouldn't kick her out of bed if she just happened to crawl in there with him. No, he'd made it pretty clear he was uncomfortable with the idea of peeping spirits. She didn't blame him; it was a bit weird for her, too.

Okay, you have to relax, she told herself, **relax and clear your mind**. That reminded her of Amethyst's guided meditation; well, it couldn't hurt to give it a try. Settling back on her pillows and focusing her attention on her breath, she pictured a golden meadow with sun-kissed grasses and colorful wildflowers gently swaying with the faint, freshly scented breeze. It was peaceful here where nothing was expected of her other than to just be in the moment. Slowly, the tension drained out of her body as her mind calmed and she drifted off to sleep.

Chapter Twenty-Two

When Tyler wandered into the kitchen the next morning, Julie handed him a cup of coffee and the plate of pancakes she'd kept warming in the oven for him. Judging by the bags under his eyes, he hadn't slept well either; and she wickedly hoped she'd had something to do with it. It was only fair. Since she'd already eaten, Julie dropped a kiss on the top of his head and went into the studio to finalize the first batch of prints from her latest series of photographs.

In Photoshop, she selected an image of Gustavia gazing directly into one of the mirrors while the others repeated her reflection from different angles, duplicated then cropped it to remove a small flare in the lower corner. Next, she selected the central image of her friend and, using layer masks, experimented with varying degrees of transparency until Gustavia's face took on a ghostlike quality. She reduced the effect around the eyes to make them appear more intense, then left the rest of the image alone. Satisfied with the outcome, she watermarked the image and emailed a copy to Saul at the gallery to get his opinion, and then went looking for Tyler, finding him upstairs in the library finishing up some work of his own.

They combed the library shelves looking for a copy of **The Magic Garden**, just to rule it out as a possibility and, when they didn't find one, chalked it off the list.

"What next?" Tyler asked.

"We were going to look for a copy of great-grandfather's will in those boxes of papers up in the attic. I do remember Grams looking at a set of building plans when she was setting up the museum; if there is any hidden space, it might show up on those."

Nestled into the central section of the house, above the main hallway, the attic area was quite small. The room was crudely finished with only two bare bulbs to beat back the dimness; it wouldn't take them long to look through its contents. Julie explained Grams had used file boxes to store all of her papers, so they were well organized. Originals of some documents were kept either in a safe or with her attorney to protect against fire or other catastrophe. Thanks to Estelle's organizational skills, they quickly found the architectural drawings for the house and the folder containing a copy of Julius' will, but there were some boxes of older documents that had never been sorted. If there were any records of purchases made by Julius, these boxes might hold them. The cramped, windowless space was not the ideal place to sort papers, so they carried the boxes down to the kitchen table and began spreading them out.

The smaller of the two boxes contained family correspondence and other papers relating to family history. As they looked through its contents, they surmised that this was part of the source for the family history that had brought the two of them together. Chances were good that they wouldn't find any new information there, so they set that box aside and concentrated on the other.

This box was full of exactly what they thought they were looking for, receipts and bills. Tyler suggested the logical approach of sorting them first by date. They had a fair idea of the time period that would most likely yield anything useful, so this seemed like the best way to start the process of elimination.

Without looking too closely at each paper, they spent half an hour sorting them into piles by the year. When that was done, they worked backward from the year of Julius's death looking for anything that might generate a lead. It was a bit like looking for a needle in a needle stack; even the most innocuous-seeming receipt might be a clue.

"Hey," Tyler said," have you noticed that Julius wasn't a big spender? We know he had a lot of money and that he sunk a portion of it into remodeling the house, more into his other inventions; but he did not seem to be in any financial crisis when he died. It might be that he kept a stack of cash in some hidey-hole."

"Your guess is as good as mine, and he's not talking. Have you found any bank books or statements? Or canceled checks? It seems odd that no one ever saw a contract detailing the amount he was paid for his invention; maybe his banking records would shed some light. Grams never talked about his money; I don't think she thought there was any left."

"So far, no banking documents; but dead ends just help us cross off possibilities."

Frustration made Julie want to stomp and scream, but she pulled it in and controlled her emotions. "So we're looking we-don't-know-where for we-don't-exactly-know-what; and the only clue we have is to find some magic, light-bringing garden that may or may not be a garden at all; and to use a key that I don't even want to think about right now. Seems like that's the situation we've been in from the beginning. What possibilities have we actually crossed off?"

She was cute when she got cranky. Tyler knew better than to voice that particular thought aloud. So, instead, he picked up the house plans and looked for a clear space to lay them out. Finding none on the table, he carried the sheets to the counter. "You keep looking through the receipts, and maybe I'll have better luck with these." Of course, if what they were searching for were small enough, it was unlikely he'd find any space on the plans; that was another thought that he kept to himself. "Keep an eye out for repair bills or anything to do with building or carpentry."

He heard her mumble something that sounded like **I freaking hate wild goose** and was glad that his back was turned so that she couldn't see him grinning like an idiot. Concentrating on Julius' rooms first, he called up his memory of the bedroom and compared it to the dimensions on the plans. They seemed to add up. Same thing for the living area and connected bathroom. There was nothing anywhere in the plans to indicate that there might be a hidden passageway so, next, he looked at the library. Nothing stood out there, either. It looked like one more dead end.

Rejoining Julie, he picked up the stack of papers dated five years before Julius' death, and it occurred to him that he should make a timeline. He went and retrieved a notebook from his computer bag and began to draw one out.

"Julie, do you have even a ballpark idea how much money Julius made from the sale of his invention? It might help us narrow down the possibilities."

"No, not really; Grams believed he'd squandered it all away. According to the plaque in the museum, he invested heavily in those contraptions but with almost no return. Royalties from the second invention that he sold still come in from time to time. There was a trust set up to pay the taxes. Until he told me himself, I wouldn't have thought he had anything to stash away except for the notes and drawings of his inventions; and, to be honest, none of us ever cared to look for those."

"Could they be valuable?"

"I doubt it."

They'd already learned from the boxes of paperwork that Julius hadn't lived what anyone would consider an extravagant lifestyle. He'd made a few changes to the house and spent a fair amount to commission those four stained-glass windows, but the bulk of his spending had been on his workshop and materials to use there. If he'd left some kind of legacy for his family—and Julie had to believe that he wouldn't have remained here in spirit form if he hadn't—it had been done on the quiet.

"Aside from the family pieces that we think he still had, Kat said stocks or bonds would have been registered and found during probate, which leaves precious metals, gems or art. Maybe rare coins or stamps. All of these would leave a paper trail of some kind. If he paid cash for them and hid the receipts along with the valuables...well...we'd be in the situation we find ourselves in right now. There would be another problem if he converted money to gold.

In 1933 the gold reform act made it illegal for the average American citizen to own more than a small amount. If he had any gold then, he'd have had to turn it in unless it was in the form of coins already recognized as collectible which were exempted."

Rubbing a hand across her forehead, Julie appreciated the depth of his knowledge. "It's all speculation at this point. This whole thing is ridiculous. I keep wondering why he would go to the trouble of hiding something from his own family. I know he and my grandfather didn't get along, but that doesn't seem like a good reason to keep his own wife from living comfortably."

"Do you know anything about their relationship?"

"Not a lot; Grams said Mary Lou was a simple woman who would rather spend time in her flower beds than anywhere else. She was the one who maintained the formal garden and insisted the space remain ornamental while teaching the Weeping Widows the finer points of growing vegetables in other parts of the property. Grams also said she would have been easily influenced by Edward; she was devoted to her son."

"So, if she had known where to find the valuables, she would probably have turned everything over to him. That seems a good reason why Julius was so secretive. What about your Grams and Edward's relationship? Did she ever talk about him?"

Julie sighed, "I think it was complicated. They were only married a short time before he went to war. She never said anything negative about him or about her marriage, but I always got the impression there was more than just the sadness of losing him."

She sat quietly for a few moments, lost in the memories of her grandmother and her own losses before pulling her attention back to the present.

"None of this helps us figure out where to look. You didn't see anything in the plans?"

"No," Tyler answered, "but that doesn't mean anything; a coffee can full of gold coins or a stamp collection wouldn't take up much space at all. They could be sealed up in a wall, or in the false bottom of a cabinet."

"And here I was hoping we might find a secret passage that opened by poking a hidden button in the fireplace trim or something." Julie smiled though she was feeling a bit trapped. Whatever was hidden needed to be found, if only to gain some peace for her great-grandfather; but the search seemed to have stalled.

"C'mon," Julie led Tyler outside, "let's get outside, take a walk, get some fresh air, and give this thing a rest for an hour."

Holding hands, they strolled through the formal gardens and followed a well-worn path into the forest. This was one of Julie's favorite places to hike; she enjoyed the sounds here in the woods: the rustling of the trees as the wind brushed their branches, the birdsong that celebrated life. As they walked, they talked about anything except treasure or ghostly visitors. Julie learned Tyler's parents lived an hour away, and he had two brothers and a sister. She envied him a bit for growing up in a larger family.

Since he knew all the sordid details of her breakup, she felt entitled to ask about his romantic past. It turned out he'd had one serious relationship that struggled, then finally couldn't survive the amount of travel he did for his job. After four years of hotel living, he admitted to being tired of the lifestyle; but Julie sensed there was more to the story, and he wasn't ready to talk about it.

When he pulled her into his arms, her heart skipped a beat then began to race as his mouth covered hers. He tasted of summer and sunlight, but with an edge of fire underneath; and all she wanted to do was to get closer. And closer still. Leaves rustled in the light breeze that whispered across heated skin as his hands crept under the edge of her tank, sliding it up as he caressed her back, gently soothing the taut muscles. When his mouth left hers, and he laid a trail of kisses down her neck, she tilted her head back to offer him better access. Every thought flew out of her head except for the need to touch his skin.

She ran like fine wine through his veins, intoxicating, drugging his senses until there was nothing left but his need to possess her, to bring her pleasure. This was not the time or the place, so he gently eased back even though he wanted nothing more than to pull her down to lie with him on the soft forest floor. Her soft moan of protest nearly undid him, but the last thing he wanted was to be her rebound relationship, so there was no way he was going to rush this. "Not here, not now," he whispered. "But soon."

Julie couldn't speak; she could hardly breathe. She knew it wasn't fair to compare them, but Logan had never made her feel like this. Thank God she'd found out about him in time. This need was so much deeper and truer than anything she'd ever felt before. What was she thinking? Only a matter of days she'd known him, and she already thought she was falling for Tyler. It was crazy, but she didn't want to resist; she wanted to plunge headlong into whatever might come. She wanted to throw caution to the wind, exactly as Grams had suggested.

Chapter Twenty-Three

Tyler answered the door when Gustavia arrived, and one look at her caused his eyebrows to raise in surprise. She was wearing jeans, a t-shirt, and, other than two or three small crystals woven into her braids, she wore no jewelry. It was like seeing Clark Kent when you expected Superman.

"Hey, what's with the normal-wear?" he asked.

Gustavia looked behind him to see if Julie was within earshot then pulled him outside for a whispered conference. "I'm going to set up some booby traps in case that boob shows up here; it's easier to climb stepladders in jeans than in skirts."

With a twinkle in his eyes, Tyler listened as she told him her plan. It seemed she'd gotten the idea from the **Home Alone** movies. She wasn't sure if Julie would approve but intended to go ahead either way, and she had another surprise coming that might not be welcome.

Back inside, Tyler gave Julie a quick goodbye kiss that had Gustavia nearly dancing in delight. This was the kind of man her friend should be with, not that arrogant goon, Logan. The minute he was gone, she grabbed the grinning Julie in a fierce hug. "I'm so happy for you."

"You know what? So am I. It just feels right; he feels right."

Gustavia brewed them a pot of herbal tea before settling on the couch and pressing Julie for information on Tyler.

"I had a reading with Kat, and she said there would be a love triangle, but we weren't sure if it meant you or me. I'm texting Ammie to pick her up on

the way here; you need the reading
you never got.

"Amethyst is coming over? How did
that happen?"

"She's bringing you a present."
Gustavia bent her head to quickly type
off a text, then hit send.

Julie was suspicious, her friend was
hiding something. She had a tell. It
wasn't something that often happened
because Gustavia rarely prevaricated.
It made her a lousy poker player. But
when she began rubbing the material at
the hem of her t-shirt between her
fingers, Julie knew. Between her
clothing choices and the determined
look on her face, Julie didn't even

bother to ask. Whatever was happening was already a done deal, so why waste the time? Besides, there was something else going on, Julie could tell. Under the surface, her friend was sad, the kind of sad that usually came after being around her family.

"Which one of them was it?"

"Hmm?"

"I know that look; you've heard from one of your family members. Zack, I'd imagine, since I can see a little mad to go along with the sad."

"He showed up at my place last night."

"Well, that's new, and I'm sorry since it probably had to do with Logan. That makes it my fault."

"It was weird. It felt like he was trying—and we didn't have a blowout or anything—but it still didn't end on a great note. He said he'd bought my books, even sounded like he was proud of me, then turned around and asked me if I'd had Grams' paintings appraised because they could be worth money. Monetary value is not always the most important thing."

"I understand, but it sounds like he meant well. I've thought if I couldn't find another way, I might sell one her paintings to pay for the new windows."

"No, I get that; and I know what it would mean for you to have to part with one. I feel the same way, and that's what he didn't understand. How do you explain to someone who has always had love and acceptance from their parents what it feels like to be on the outside looking in? Grams meant the world to me; she was the only real mother I've ever known. If those paintings were worth millions, it wouldn't matter to me." Tears filled Gustavia's eyes, but she blinked them back and made an effort to change the subject before things got even more maudlin than they already were. "Speaking of Grams and millions, any progress?"

"No, not even the tiniest bit." Julie ran a hand across her forehead as though trying to wipe away a headache, the kind caused by frustration. "We spent a lot of time speculating, but nothing concrete. I think we are just missing something obvious. I hate to keep repeating it, but I have this pesky feeling I should know exactly what the magic garden is, that I've seen it written somewhere; but whenever I get close, it just keeps slipping away."

Gustavia nodded her understanding, and changing the subject, made small talk until the doorbell chimed. She hurried ahead of Julie to open the door for Amethyst and Kat. She'd barely finished turning the knob when the door was forcefully pushed open, and a blur of tawny fur shot past her heading straight for Julie. Gustavia turned just in time to see her friend borne to the floor by 90 pounds of excited dog. Ammie rushed in, broken leash in hand, followed more sedately by Kat swinging her cane and being led by the sounds the dog was making.

"What is this? A Wookie?" Julie demanded as the dog voiced something halfway between a growl and howl, then ran its rather large tongue across her face. "Get off me, you moose." She pushed the dog aside so she could sit up. The boxer danced away—but only for a moment—then returned to try and climb into her lap while staring adoringly into Julie's eyes. Amethyst reached out a hand to help Julie up off the floor. "This is Lola. We thought you could use some extra protection, so I borrowed her from a friend who runs a shelter. She's a sweet dog; she's just young and tends to be a bit, well, exuberant."

"I can see that," was the dry reply. "Did it occur to any of you to ask me first?"

Gustavia grinned, "It occurred to us you might say no, so we decided not to bother." As always, Gustavia thought it was better to ask for forgiveness than permission. "Lola needs a temporary home; you need someone to help guard the house. It seemed like a good match. She's just on loan for a few weeks, unless you get attached and want to keep her." She grinned at Julie's narrowed-eyed scowl.

Resisting Lola, though, was a nearly impossible task; her warm brown eyes could melt an iceberg. When she left Julie's side to gently nudge against Kat's leg, as though instinctively knowing she needed to proceed carefully around this particular human, Julie was hooked. "Okay, she can stay."

Ammie exchanged a triumphant grin with Gustavia, and the two of them went back to the car to carry in Lola's things. And, for a dog, she had an unexpected amount of baggage: a large bed, water, and food bowls, several toys, some treats and a huge bag of kibble were all piled by the door.

While Julie was getting the rundown from Ammie on Lola's current routine, Gustavia quietly excused herself to begin putting her plan for a second line of defense into action. Even though she knew the house inside and out, she had never assessed its potential for breaking and entering until now. Even to her untrained eye, the old windows—though charming in style—were easily breached, and the back door lock system would only deter the honest. If she was sure it wouldn't start an epic fight, she'd have already called an alarm company and a locksmith and paid for the installations herself. She'd already had this discussion with Julie and been summarily shut down. **So, she thought, booby traps will have to do.**

She was so absorbed with putting her plan into action that Julius had to clear his ghostly throat several times before she heard him. To her credit, she took his presence in stride by greeting him with a big smile, once he'd gotten her attention. He had been watching her with avid curiosity, then discerning her goal, had decided to help.

"You any good with a hammer?" he asked.

Gustavia grinned. Over the last few years, she had regularly taken part in building homes through Habitat for Humanity. That experience helped make her comfortable with a variety of hand and power tools. She'd even dragged Julie along a few times. What they had learned had helped the two of them do some of the more minor repairs to Hayward House, and even to build a potting shed in Gustavia's back yard from some reclaimed materials. They had delayed the need for a whole new roof for another year or so and had repaired the worst of the old windows, but it was time for new, and that was a significant expense. For right now, the concern was how easily Logan could jack one of these relics open.

Julius explained to her that since these were single hung windows, it would be simple to block them closed by wedging slats of wood into the opening above the bottom window. With the windows held closed, Logan would have to break the glass to gain entry, thereby reducing the stealth factor.

"What do you think about leaving one window unblocked and setting up a trap for him?"

"I think you have a devious mind, gypsy girl," Julius answered with an appraising look, "You remind me a bit of Estelle."

Flattered, Gustavia said, "I can't think of a better compliment than that; Estelle was one of my heroes. She had guts."

"That she did and still does. We have had some ideas that fit in perfectly with your own. Now listen..." and he outlined a plan that made Gustavia do her favorite victory dance. Just let that moron try to break in here; he would get what was coming to him and then some.

With Julius directing her, it didn't take Gustavia long to cut some slats that she could staple into place and secure the downstairs windows. Next, he showed her how to rig the rickety lock on the back door so Logan would not be able to jimmy it open. Then Julius sent her out to his workshop where she found the bits and pieces she needed to set up a trip wire on the one unsecured window sill; any attempt to gain entry would lift the latch that opened the door leading to the kitchen and let Lola into the room.

Finally, with a wicked grin on her face, Gustavia went to her car, grabbed a plastic bag and, as Julius watched, layered the section of the floor in front of the window with squeaky toys. If there was one thing Lola could not resist, it was the sound of a squeaky toy; one squawk would bring her running and barking from just about anywhere in the house. Julius would also be listening; if Logan managed to get inside, he was going to get the surprise of his life. The only thing Gustavia regretted was she didn't have time to set up a camera, because she knew this could easily turn into a video-worthy moment.

Satisfied with her efforts, and still armed with the slats and staple gun, Gustavia made her way back into the house where she ignored both Julie's questioning look and her protests, and secured each of the downstairs windows then led the rest of the group out the back of the kitchen to show them her handiwork.

Chapter Twenty-Four

Downing his umpteenth cup of coffee
for the day, Zack ran a hand through
his hair in frustration. Logan was a step
ahead of him, had been from the start.
Still, there were a few more lines to tug
on, and the evidence was beginning to
pile up. He had left a trail—maybe it
wasn't a mile wide, but it was there—
and Zack could see it becoming clearer

and clearer. He had enough to put Logan away, but his gut told him there was more to find.

That wasn't all his gut was telling him. He figured Julie knew more than she thought she did; there had to be something, some detail, that would help him run the slimy little crook to ground. Discreet inquiry had proved Logan had not been at his office for several days; he'd bolted. The question was whether he had cut his losses and run or was hanging around waiting for a chance to make trouble. If he had to bet, Zack would pick the latter; it would explain this feeling he kept having that the other shoe had yet to drop.

First thing tomorrow, he decided, he would go and talk to Julie. Eloise would probably be there since, if he remembered correctly, it was her night to keep Julie company. After their not-quite-a-fight last night, he thought having a bit of a buffer between he and his sister was probably a good idea, anyway. Sitting outside of her house for an entire night had given him a lot of time to think, and he had come to the conclusion it was well past time they patched things up between them.

He had been surprised and somewhat blindsided by the depth of feeling he had experienced while spending time with her. Zack finally admitted to himself that he loved his sister, pure and simple. It was impossible to shove those feelings down anymore; he missed having her in his life; they'd been important to each other as children, and he hoped she felt the same way. It had seemed as though she did, at least for the first part of the evening.

With these goals firmly in mind, he locked up his office. Right now, he had two thoughts in his head: a quick meal and getting some sack time. He'd been running without sleep for more than 36 hours, and it was time to recharge.

At the same moment Zack was locking his office door, Logan was flat on his belly in the woods near Julie's house peering through the eyepiece of a high powered set of binoculars and swearing a blue streak under his breath. He'd expected Julie to be there alone; but instead, through the windows, he could see several women laughing and talking in front of the fireplace. Where had all these women come from? She didn't have that many friends; he had picked her precisely because she had so few connections; it made his job a lot easier. And, as he always did, he blamed Gustavia; these had to be her cronies, especially the one with purple hair.

If he had seen Lola snoozing contentedly on her new bed, he would have gone ballistic, but he didn't. Instead, he weaseled his way back out of the low brush and hiked back to his campsite. Julius followed, listening in on Logan's internal dialog and growing more and more certain the young man's sanity was eroding: his thoughts were still coherent, but chaotic and becoming darkly violent. Still, underneath the seething anger, there was something of that keen mind left, maybe enough to keep him from tipping over the edge; but only if someone could find a way to reach him, and Julius didn't think he was the one for the job.

"**It sounds** like Logan is a total loser, and you're way better off without him. Julie wins the bad boyfriend prize," Amethyst declared with the total conviction that comes from being slightly buzzed.

They killed the second bottle of wine.

"Hey, I'm not the only one who's had some bad boyfriends; Gustavia dated at least five of the seven dwarfs: Happy, Sleepy, Grumpy, Sneezy and Dopey. Happy was nice enough, but not too deep. Sleepy spent a lot of time in bed. Grumpy lasted less than a week with his bad attitude, and Sneezy had the worst hay fever I have ever seen. His nose was always red and runny."

"What about Dopey? Dumb or always high?" Ammie asked.

"A little bit of both," Julie replied with a smirk.

"Well, you dated the dwarfs lesser known cousins: Arty, Farty, and Smarty."

Amethyst snorted at that one. "Okay, I'll bite. Describe please."

"Arty was an art major who spent hours talking about Rene Magritte. He was all about the **this is not a pipe** thing. Smarty had a high IQ and asked everyone their number. He even used it to insult people. If he thought you weren't smart, he called you a **ninety**. But, Farty, he was a rare find. He thought he could control his farts, and his goal was to fart the alphabet before the end of the year."

"Eww," Ammie and Kat expressed disgust in unison. "How do you fart the alphabet? No one can do that."

"He was totally convinced he could do it. The facial expressions he made were priceless, though." Gustavia giggled at the memory.

Julie held up both hands in surrender. "Yeah, I broke up with him the day he swore he did the **W** and cried about it."

Ammie and Kat both burst out laughing.

"Then, Gustavia dated a whole series of twisted nursery rhyme characters.

Let's see. There was Little Jack Horny and Wee Willie Winky. No explanation necessary."

Gustavia shrugged to indicate her innocence.

"Then came Tom, Tom the Plumber's Son."

Just say no to crack, Gustavia quoted as everyone continued to laugh. "Julie cured it, though. She dropped a quarter down there and squealed, **Oooh, look, a piggy bank**."

"Oh, and we can't forget Peter, Peter Garlic Eater or my own personal favorite: Little Boy Blue." Julie waggled her eyebrows with a wicked grin.

Gustavia screamed with laughter. "Oh, my Goddess, I had forgotten him."

This time Kat had to ask. "What was his thing?"

"Blue was his favorite color--in women's panties."

"So, he wanted you to wear blue panties all the time?"

"Not me, him."

"Stop, you have to stop before I wet myself." Ammie rushed toward the bathroom laughing so hard she could barely see where she was going.

"He was almost as bad as Nudie Rudy. It's okay to give your jiggly bits an airing whenever you want; as long as you do it in the privacy of your own home. But keep your snake in the

basket when you're at mine, please."
Julie's lips wrinkled in disgust.

More screams of laughter.

"You two are horrible."

"I'm sure we were no picnic for some of them, either. We went through some weird phases of our own."

Gustavia nodded emphatically. "Yeah, there was the **we are only going to date older men** phase. Julie thought for a moment. "Was that before or after the **we are only going to date younger men** phase? The theory behind that one was we figured we could train them up the way we wanted them."

"How did that work out for you?" Amethyst smirked as though she'd been there herself.

"About like you'd think."

"I can't remember them all, but there was a pissed off rocker phase and the one where we kissed everyone on both cheeks and wore berets."

"But enough about us; you guys must have a story or two. Spill."

Amethyst kicked it off. "Let's see. I don't think mine were quite so funny, but there was the guy who had more hair on his back than Sasquatch. I could have lived with that, but he made this weird humming sound every time he kissed me. It creeped me out after a while."

They all agreed this was a sensible reaction, as they passed around the third wine bottle.

"And there was another one who had cold feet. Not the fear of commitment kind but the oh-my-God-did-you-smuggle-a-block-of-ice-into-bed kind. I think he had a circulation problem."

She went on. "But the worst one was this guy who told me he loved me just the way I was and then spent four years trying to turn me into Nancy Normal. I actually had the bad taste to marry that one."

Surprised she had not known this about her friend, Gustavia offered a hug of sympathy then let Amethyst finish her story. The laughing was over; this was clearly a painful memory, and probably way past time to let go of it.

"It was right after high school. We thought we were so grown up, and even though our parents warned us not to, we eloped. He said my not being conventional was one of the things he loved most about me. But he couldn't find work, so he took a job in his dad's insurance agency; and, before long, he was acting more like his father than like himself." She sniffed back a tear. "He started wearing suits and ties and asking me to **tone it down** in public. Then he asked me if I could stop seeing auras and I left. Just packed my stuff and ran one day while he was at work."

"He was an idiot." Gustavia tended to get hotly angry whenever she perceived injustice.

Ammie's tone was sad. "No, he was just young. We both were."

Kat spoke. "I don't have any stories. I was fifteen the first time I saw spirits. By the time I was sixteen, I was blind. It seemed like too much of a burden to put on anyone so, I've never even been in a relationship."

Tears of sympathy streamed down Gustavia's cheeks as she sat down next to Kat and took her hand. "Oh sweetie, that's so sad."

A look was passed between the other three. A look that plainly said they intended to remedy the situation one way or another. Let the matchmaking begin.

"I didn't mean to bring you all down," Ammie said as she elbowed Gustavia lightly. Gustavia took the hint, and with a wicked glint in her eye, proceeded to out Julie's newly forming relationship. "Julie kissed Tyler."

"Hah!" Kat nearly shouted with triumph.

"Fine," Amethyst replied as she grabbed her purse, pulled out a ten-dollar bill and passed it to Kat. "Fine, you win. I should know better than to bet with you anyway."

Eyes widening in surprise Julie said, "You bet on whether I would get together with Tyler?"

"No," Kat laughed. "We bet on how long it would take for Tyler to make his move; the two of you getting together was inevitable."

Julie frowned. "I don't understand. How do you figure? I thought he had a thing for Gustavia until just before he kissed me."

Amethyst said, "Oh honey, how many excuses does a man have to make to spend time with you? You've known him for, what--a week or so? And he volunteers to sleep over in a haunted house to protect you from your possibly psycho ex?"

"Well, when you put it like that, it doesn't sound terribly appealing. Besides, I've only known you and Kat for about a week, and here the two of you are, ready to sleep over in a haunted house to protect me from my possibly psycho ex."

Amethyst rolled her eyes. "That's because we love you."

Julie was overwhelmed at the simple statement; the matter of fact way it was made allowed for no mistake that the sentiment was genuine. As she looked at the other three women, the burden of losing the last of her family eased a little. She had a new family.

Estelle's heart soared; the girl had a good solid circle of women in her life, even if they had some odd ideas at times. And hey—as a ghost, was she really in any position to have an opinion on whether auras were real or not? There was a click that sounded faintly bell-like as she realized one of her objectives in remaining earthbound had just been met.

She was just about to zip out of the room when Lola—who had been sleeping quietly on her bed—opened one lazy eye and looked right at her, then the other eye opened. As the dog lifted her head, Estelle could see Lola was considering whether to raise the alarm, so she hissed a low-pitched shushing sound while sending reassuring thoughts. This was enough to quiet the dog. Lola tilted her head to the left as if appraising the apparition before her, then gave her best doggy grin before settling down and going back to sleep. Relieved that she had not created a scene, Estelle sped out to the gazebo roof to find Julius.

Chapter Twenty-Five

Over the next two weeks or so, they made no progress on the search, and it began to look like they never would. Julie's life settled into a pattern; and, as the days wore on, with no further sign from Logan, everyone began to assume he had left town for good. Amethyst and Kat took occasional turns sleeping over; but, thankfully, it had been decided Julie was safe enough, with Julius keeping an ear out and Lola in the house, to stay alone during the day. Grateful for her friends, she was equally grateful for the time alone.

Tamara had recommended Julie to her friend Allison, a clothing designer, and Julie spent several days shooting her new line. The work was interesting, paid well, and artistic enough to be satisfying on that level, so Julie agreed to take on several more commercial commissions. With the extra money, she could probably pay for new windows by next spring.

Left on her own, she would have chosen to forget all about missing family fortune, but Gustavia and Tyler wouldn't let it go; plus, with Julius popping in every now and then to see if there had been any progress, and looking more anxious every time, it was clear he wasn't going to let it go either. His visits were fairly brief since, without having Kat as an available conduit, it took a lot of his energy to speak; though Julie noticed when he remained quiet and only partially materialized, Julius could spend more time glowering at her than she cared to deal with. At least he and Estelle had both agreed to ring the doorbell before they appeared. It was especially important for them to give her some warning now that there were more clients in the studio.

Gustavia stayed in touch with Zack; the two were no longer actively sparring off of each other at every possible opportunity, but they were still uneasy when in the same room. His frustration at not being able to run Logan to ground made him more short-tempered than normal. At his insistence, Gustavia had a state-of-the-art security system installed in her tiny cottage.

It was Kat who suggested a Saturday night brainstorming session if everyone was agreeable; some of the spirit's anxiety had begun transferring itself to her, and she was feeling the pressure of the passing time. Everyone showed up for dinner and, after scarfing down some pizza, they all trooped up to Julius' rooms.

"I've said since the first night I stayed here that it felt like I was missing some small, but vital, clue." Tyler pulled out his voice recorder and keyed it back to the beginning of Estelle's description of Julius' death. "Maybe if we give this a listen, something will jump out at us." He hit the play button.

"Once he was gone, we put things back to rights; and, after that, Mary Lou never changed a thing. She kept it as a shrine after he died." Then after a pause of several seconds, "It was here in this bed that he sat up with the firelight glittering in his eyes, stared over our heads and said, **Use the key with the magic garden; they will show you the hiding place. Follow the light.** Then he looked right at me and said, **don't forget. Key--magic garde**n. He was upset, agitated. At the time I thought it was just restlessness. In his last weeks, he was in a considerable amount of pain, and his muscles twitched a lot, but I think he was gesturing toward something to his left."

Kat gave a little shiver at hearing Estelle's voice for the first time and knowing it had come out of her own mouth. The short clip played through and, for long seconds, nobody spoke.

"You're right; there's something there, but I can't quite put my finger on it." Gustavia was thoughtful as she tried to picture the scene in her mind: the man, ravaged by illness, surrounded by family.

"Play it again," Ammie ordered. She'd caught something in the wording that didn't sound right but lost it again.

They listened closely for a second—then a third—time before Ammie looked up, a slow smile spreading across her face, "The firelight. There's no fireplace in this room," she stated as comprehension dawned on her.

"That's it!" Tyler all but shouted. "Julius said something about the fire going day and night, but I didn't catch on."

"He died in this bed, but not in this room." Julie moved into the living room of the suite with everyone following her. "They must have moved his bed in here." She stood, facing the fireplace in the approximate position she thought the bed would have occupied. "If the bed was here and he was trying to point to something on his left, it would have to be the stained glass window."

As one, they all turned toward the vividly colored window with its floral motif. Then Julie bent to read the engraving on the small, brass plaque

514

affixed to the wall below. She turned back to the others, eyes widened in surprise, "it's called the **Magic Garden**," she said. "It has been here all the time, big as life and right in front of us."

Kat remained where she was as the others rushed to the window to examine it in detail. It was a spectacular work of art with its brightly colored flowers, each petal delicately detailed, set in an oak frame elaborately carved with leaves and vines. Across the top of the frame, the word **solstice** was etched deeply into the wood.

As Tyler neared the window, he saw, mounted on the right-hand side, two seemingly decorative, wrought iron brackets each holding an L-shaped rod that laid flat against the wall. One simple touch had the rods swinging, hinge-like, to rest against the trim with the long end of the L sticking out about four inches. The end of the upper rod had been hammered into a square shape while the lower one remained rounded. At first, he thought they might have once been part of a shutter or drapery system, but he realized whatever was attached to them would, when closed, stand at right angles to the window rather than cover the glass; so neither option made much sense.

Gustavia, always sensitive to the feelings of others, realized Kat had been relegated to the sidelines and, pulling her back into the group, described the window while guiding her friend's hand over the raised leading strips between the glass pieces. It was Kat who, while running her braille-trained fingers over the carved frame, found two tiny, raised key emblems among the vines near each of the brackets.

"So, we're supposed to **use the magic garden with the key**; maybe these brackets have something to do with the key," Julie said.

"Ammie, can you see anything?" Gustavia asked as she poked and prodded the raised wooden keys.

Amethyst refocused her eyes, "No, not anymore. We were so excited that whatever residual aura might have been there, we have overlaid with our own."

"Let's get logical." Tyler got out his notepad, sat on the couch, and motioned for the others to join him. "We've got the first part of the puzzle, and we know the key has to interact with the window." He jotted this down on the paper. "And, those carved keys were not placed randomly; they have to mean something. There are two symbols. But Julius only used the word

key not **keys,** so we know we are probably looking for a single key; one that can somehow be used with a window."

"Following that logic, it's not the kind of key that fits in a lock, but maybe something more like a map key. If that's the case, it was probably thrown out years ago."

"No, I don't think so. Julius put a considerable amount of effort into creating a hiding place and having the window installed; he would make sure the key was something that would stay in the house, with the family. It's here somewhere."

"Oh! I have an idea," Gustavia said with a wicked gleam in her eye, "what if we reenact his death scene."

"That is positively morbid," Julie wrinkled her nose in disgust.

"No, it's genius." Kat chimed in. "If we could get the ghosts to cooperate, we might get another clue. It can't hurt to try." She quieted her mind, reaching out psychically to see if either of the two spirits were around. There was a faint answering echo from Estelle: "I have already shown you; think about what you have seen."

Kat opened her eyes, holding up her hand to forestall any questions; she explored her memory and, after a moment, decided she understood the message. "Estelle was able to show me a fragment of her memory from the day Julius died, enough to see where Julius was looking and his hand when he gestured. I'm pretty sure I can guide you into the right positions, then it will be up to you to figure out what he was looking at."

Rather than dismantling the bed and moving it, they decided the sofa would make a decent enough stand-in, and it was already in place. It just needed to be angled toward the fireplace. Tyler would play Julius. Kat would direct the movements of Julie, Gustavia, and Amethyst based on what she had seen in her brief glimpse through Estelle's memory.

"Okay, Tyler, just lie down; and, Julie, you sit on the right side of the bed; Amethyst you are on the left; and, Gustavia, you stand on the right, just by his head. Then, Tyler, you sit up and look just above Julie's head and slightly to the right. What do you see?"

"Fireplace. I'm looking right at the mantel, but that can't be the key. The gesture to the left lines up with the window, so that makes sense."

Gustavia linked arms with Amethyst, and the two of them approached the fireplace and began removing the photographs from the mantel. Being the two tallest of the group, it fell to

Tyler and Gustavia to lift the mirror in its ornate frame down from the wall. Before they even had a chance to look at the mirror, Julie noticed something about the wall.

"Hey, look," she said. "There used to be something else that hung here." She pointed to the darker square of wallpaper. "I can't believe it; another dead end."

"No, it's not a dead end; we just have to search the house for something that fits that size. Wait here, I'll be back." Gustavia ran from the room to return a few minutes later with a measuring tape that she used on the darker square of wallpaper.

Tyler jotted down the dimensions, and they started measuring the artwork beginning with the second-floor bedrooms. Being the home of an artist, Hayward house had no shortage of pieces to measure. Julie was able to rule out some of the pieces because she knew Estelle had painted them after Julius' death. The second floor yielded two possibilities, but it wasn't until they went downstairs and walked into the living room that Julie realized what she should have known all along. It had to be the painting of Julius that had been hanging over the fireplace for as long as she could remember. She stopped and pointed, "That's it," she breathed.

Gustavia told Kat in an undertone what they had found. Tyler stepped up to take a closer look and turned with an excited gleam in his eye, "It's signed—and you won't believe this—the artist's name seems to be **A. Key**." He was unprepared for the pitch and volume of the feminine screams that erupted upon hearing his comment.

In the painting, Julius was posed formally, standing next to his note-covered desk in the library. Behind him were the familiar rows of books and to one side sat a table covered with pieces of an invention in progress. Julie stepped up onto the hearth to take a closer look. Sure enough. The painting was signed by **Andrew Key**, with both the **A** and **Key** in much larger script than the remaining letters in **Andrew**. Her heart sped up, and her hands began to tremble just a little. This was it, the key. Now, how was she supposed to use it?

Slowly and carefully, she and Tyler lifted the large portrait down from the wall while Gustavia and Amethyst spread some towels over the table to protect both it and the painting. They laid it face down on the towels. At first glance, there was nothing remotely key-like about what they saw, at least from the back.

"Do you think we should pull off the backing?" Amethyst asked.

"Not yet; let's flip it over and take a look at the front first."

Now that the painting was face up, Kat ran her hand over the skillfully carved frame. "Here's another carved key," she said as she prodded the spot with her sensitive fingers. Then she said, "Oh!" as the tiny key moved under her probing touch. There was a soft click as a round hole opened up in the side of the frame, then another as she found the second wooden key, this one opening a square hole on the lower end of the frame.

There was no need for more discussion; every one of them knew what they needed to do. Tyler picked up the painting and led the way back upstairs. No one said a word as they followed him into Julius' rooms, Kat and Gustavia arm in arm. He gestured with nothing more than a nod of his head for Julie to flip the brackets out on the right-hand side of the window, then he lifted the painting onto the brackets so that it hung at a right angle to the window.

"Now what?" Amethyst asked.

"Well, it says **solstice** here on the trim, and the window shows a summer theme. The summer solstice is only a few days away; maybe we need to somehow use the key then." Gustavia thought about it for another minute. "I hope there's a clue somewhere about when to use it because, otherwise, we are going to all be sitting here staring at the thing for an entire day."

Tyler took the portrait down from the brackets and carried it back down to the table. Where the others inspected the painting closely while Kat sat nearby petting Lola, who gazed up at her lovingly.

It was Ammie who, several minutes later, sang out, "Found it! Duh, easy when you think about it. There's a clock in the painting, upper left-hand side. Looks like it says 3:20. Seems too random to not mean anything, so that has to be it."

"You're right."

"Okay, it looks like we have a plan: on the day of the solstice, we hang the key on the brackets and see what happens at 3:20," Julie said.

"AM or PM?" Gustavia wondered.

Tyler answered firmly, "PM. **The magic garden brings the light**, so it has to be daytime."

Chapter Twenty-Six

From his favorite spot, Logan watched Julie load several framed photographs into her car. It was about time she left the house; he'd been waiting for his chance to get inside and take a look around. If Julie had seen him skulking in the brush, she might never have recognized her former fiancé, he was so changed from the man she had known. With no hope for securing the Hayward property, he'd never returned to his offices, and then, once some local yokel of a cop had come sniffing around his apartment, he decided the best thing to do was to lay low.

He had spent the past few weeks camping in the woods near Julie's place waiting for a time when the house would be empty. He hadn't shaved or showered. His normally immaculately styled hair, now a disheveled mess, stood on end where he had repeatedly run his hands through it in frustration. But, it was the fevered gleam in his eyes that Julie would have found most alien in the face she had come to know and care for. His time in the woods had chiseled away the layer of respectability Logan had always carefully maintained and allowed his true nature to show itself vividly on his face.

After she had driven away, Logan waited a few minutes to make sure Julie was gone before leaving his hiding place and striding toward the house. He'd already chosen his entry point. One window near the back door was open an inch or two, and it would be a simple matter to nudge it all the way open and crawl headfirst inside.

He felt a little resistance, but quickly had the window open and hoisted himself over the sill. He had time to see the squeaky toys littered on the floor, but not enough time to avoid them. He landed on the pile, and the toys lived up to their promise by emitting a cacophony of squealing noises.

Lola, hearing the sublime call of her favorite plaything shot through the now open kitchen door on a dead run barking at the top of her lungs. The plan had worked perfectly.

Julius sent Estelle off to fetch Tyler and then settled his energy over Lola, concentrating on forming an image of her with fierce eyes and bared teeth and on making it corporeal enough for Logan to see the friendly face turn menacing. He needn't have bothered.

Lola's sweet personality covered up a keen sense of perception, and she knew this human was a threat to her new owner and her home. Her deep barks turned to growls as she lunged at Logan with only one thought on her mind: save the house from the bad guy. Julius quickly dissipated his efforts to save energy and stepped back to enjoy the show.

Logan scrambled to his feet and, letting loose a steady stream of invective, kicked at the dog before launching himself back out the way he'd come in. He made a halfhearted attempt to close the window; but, with Lola jumping and snarling each time she saw his hand, he quickly abandoned the effort.

At this point, Julius concentrated his energy, popped the latch on the back door and nudged it open enough to let Lola out. The boxer lunged through the door and made a beeline for Logan, who ran for his life as the big dog chased him across the property. Lola, running flat out had all the grace of a newborn giraffe; but, even with her uneven gait, she quickly outmatched her prey as Julius skimmed along beside her.

Tyler looked up from his laptop as Estelle materialized in front of him and, even though he'd thought he was used to this ghost stuff by now, goosebumps broke out on his arms. Estelle spoke, "It's Logan! He's headed for the house; can you come?"

Without a moment's hesitation, Tyler snatched up his car keys and was out the door on a dead run. He calculated it would take at least three minutes to get there and, determined to shave a minute off that time, floored the accelerator. When he passed Zack about a mile from Julie's house, he was doing 65 in a 45 mph zone. Meanwhile, back at the house, Logan had just landed in the squeaky zone. Zack flipped on the lights and made a quick U-turn to follow him while calling in his plate number. When the info from the car's registration came back, Zack recognized the name and realized something was wrong. Tyler made no effort to pull over. When he turned up the drive, Zack flipped off the siren and followed. They both parked and jumped out of their cars at the same time.

"Where is she?" Zack yelled at exactly the same time as Tyler yelled, "Logan Ellis is here!" Then, hearing Lola's frantic barking in the woods off to the left of the house, both men bolted in that direction. Estelle flashed on ahead to find man, dog, and ghost in the clearing where Logan had been camping for the past few days.

The big boxer stood behind Julius— the short, spiky fur on her back and neck bristling with fury—while Logan tried, for all he was worth, to brain her with a fist-sized rock. Each time he tried to hit the dog, Julius deflected his aim, but Estelle could see her father-in-law's energy was rapidly becoming depleted. Turning back, she yelled to Tyler to hurry. Tyler and Zack broke into the clearing side by side—Zack with gun drawn—just as Logan managed to land a glancing blow on the dog's shoulder. Lola yelped in pain then twisted her head to sink her teeth into his arm.

Zack yelled, "Stop right there!" But Logan shook his arm free, with a shriek of pain and anger, then turned to race off down the path behind his tent. Before Zack and Tyler reached the spot where Lola now lay whining in pain, they heard the sound of a car motor starting up. Tyler stopped to see to the dog while Zack continued running and reached the rutted track just in time to catch a glimpse of the rear of Logan's vehicle as it disappeared down the old access road.

He managed to get a partial plate number and quickly jotted it down before returning to the clearing where he found Tyler kneeling beside Lola, running his hands over her and speaking to her in a calm, soothing voice. Estelle and Julius hovered nearby, but Zack couldn't or wouldn't see them.

Tyler looked up, "Hey, man, sorry I didn't stop. Give me the ticket; I won't argue. Tyler Kingsley. You may not remember, but we met once a few years back." He held out his hand.

"Yeah, you were doing a story on that RICO case; you probably know my sister Eloise," he said as he shook the proffered hand. Then, at Tyler's puzzled look, he added, "Gustavia, she goes by Gustavia," and he rolled his eyes.

"Oh," Tyler smiled, "now, her I know. She's amazing."

Zack arched an eyebrow at that but didn't bother to answer. He squatted down to look at Lola. "Looked like he hit her pretty hard; how bad is it?"

"She needs to go to the vet, but I think she'll be okay." He stroked the big dog's head as she gazed up him, brave but still sad-eyed. "Good girl."

Both men stood up. "You going after him?" Tyler asked.

"Not much sense in it at this point; he's long gone by now."

Lola struggled to her feet then limped a yard or so before sitting back down with a low whimper. "I think I can pick her up without causing too much pain," Tyler said.

"Give me your keys; I'll bring your car up the access road. No sense in carrying her all the way back to the house. She looks a bit heavy for that."

Tyler tossed them over, and Zack took off at a fast jog. A few minutes later, Tyler recognized the sound of his vehicle as Gustavia's brother pulled up to the makeshift campsite and left the car running while moving some things to make enough space in the back for the boxer to be comfortable. Lifting her gently, he settled her as carefully as he could, then turned to Zack appraisingly; he wasn't sure how much of the story anyone had provided the man, and he didn't want to give away any state secrets. Zack spoke first.

"That was Logan Ellis, Julie's ex, right?"

"In the flesh. Looks like he's been stalking her."

"Looks like," Zack agreed, "Guess I'll be taking a look through his home away from home while you get the dog to the vet. Here's my cell number," he handed Tyler his card, "keep me posted. I'm going to pick this place apart, and then I'll need to talk to Julie."

Tyler nodded, his face going grim as he jumped in, reversed in the small clearing, and drove off toward town.

Zack watched pensively until the taillights disappeared and then pulled out his cell phone to call his sister.

When she answered the phone, he told her in short, terse sentences what had happened and agreed to let Gustavia contact Julie with the news about Lola.

There wasn't much in the tent: a change of clothes, a sleeping bag, some food, a frying pan, a pot, and a small propane camp stove. Logan had been living rough; the inside of the tent smelled a lot like feet. If there had been anything of interest here, the jerk must have kept it in his car, the car he'd gotten away in. And that pissed Zack off no end. Still, he had a plate number. With that thought, he grabbed his cell phone to call in a BOLO. With any luck, someone would have eyes on the guy before he got away clean.

Since Julie was already in town, the call from Gustavia got her to the vet's office just as Tyler pulled up in front. Without even thinking about it, she rushed into his arms and clung for a moment before asking, "How badly is she hurt?"

"It's her shoulder. Julius held him off as long as he could. I think she'll be fine, but let's get her in there." After carefully scooping Lola out of the car, he carried her inside while her tiny stump of a tail wagged like crazy and she gave him a big sloppy kiss.

An hour or so later, after x-rays and a thorough exam, they learned Lola didn't have any broken bones, only a deeply bruised shoulder and a small cut that would heal with time, and she was released.

Zack was waiting for them when they pulled up in front of the house. One look at his grim face told Julie Logan was still in the wind.

"We found his car an hour ago, abandoned and empty. But the B and E was enough for a warrant. Do you know where he got in?" Julius had popped in on his granddaughter during the ride back from the vet's and given her the rundown, while Estelle did the same for Tyler; so they both knew exactly how and where Logan had entered the house.

"Gustavia sealed off all the windows except one," Julie explained as she led Zack back outside, "and then she set up a booby trap for him."

"Hmmph." Zack pulled out a small notepad and jotted down some notes. When he saw his sister's handiwork, he let the barest of smiles slip through his stern expression before getting back down to business. He asked Julie to give him a rundown of how she met Logan, what their relationship had been like, and describe how things had ended. She was surprised at his gentleness as he asked probing questions and elicited detailed information that she would never have thought pertinent.

By the time he was done, she could see a pattern that revealed the criminal lurking behind the man she had thought she'd loved. As Zack watched the comprehension dawning on her face and the dismay she felt for not seeing things clearly, he was thankful she had a support system in place because she was absolutely devastated.

"Do you think he's coming back? Am I safe?"

"If he is as smart as I think he is, he will go to ground and resurface somewhere with a new name. Be a bit harder now that he has a couple warrants. There's nothing for him now but revenge. He'd be stupid to go after you now. Or insane."

Comforting words if she dared to believe them, but Julie wasn't so sure.

Chapter Twenty-Seven

On June 21st, the date of the summer solstice, the afternoon sun speared through the stained glass window, diffusing through tiny shards of color, and bending, refracting through the prism set in the center of the summer garden scene. The rainbow-infused light sparkled and intensified in brilliance as it slanted across the bracketed portrait, spotlighting an area on the farthest shelves near the right-hand side of the library. The phenomenon lasted only a short time, five minutes at most, as four of the five friends stood watching, and Kat listened to Gustavia's whispered explanation.

When the spark fell dim, they stood still a moment longer reflecting on the journey that had brought them to this exact moment before turning as one and walking purposefully toward the library. If this had been a movie, the moment would have been immortalized by one of those slow-motion, wind-in-the-hair scenes.

Then, Gustavia broke the spell of solemnity by letting loose a war cry that had Kat jolting in surprise and jabbing an elbow into her friend's ribcage.

"Warn a person before you shriek like that; you scared me half to death."

"Sorry, sorry. It's just—this is amazing. Right? I mean, we're going to find something; I just know it."

Just before they entered the library, Kat sensed Estelle nearby. When the spirit whispered in her ear, "Do you want to see it?" she breathed, "Yes," and opened herself up. Estelle slid inside her like a diver entering the water with barely a ripple. It was a much different experience than before: rather than taking over her body, the spirit shared it. With that thought, her vision cleared. Julius stood behind the desk waiting for them.

Julie didn't even blink at the sight of him. "Where's Grams?" She asked.

"Right here," the answer came from Kat. Then, in her own voice, Kat said, "I'm here, too." It was eerie. Julie looked at her great-grandfather, who remained silent but waved her on. Julie grasped Tyler's hand. Together they inspected the area indicated by the painting and saw—nothing.

"Oh, you've got to be kidding," Julie could not believe her eyes. She reached out a finger running it over the edge of the molding. Totally smooth. There was nothing there. She pinned Julius with a narrow-eyed stare. "Is this your idea of a joke? Some kind of ghostly prank?"

Julius didn't answer, couldn't. Estelle spoke softly. "Julie," was all she said; but there was disappointment in her tone.

"Wait." Tyler turned and strode out of the room; Gustavia followed him while Julie took several deep breaths to try and regain control of her emotions. Tyler made his way straight back to where the painting was still attached to the brackets. For a long moment he just stood there looking at it; then he reached out and swung the portrait slightly on the hinged brackets. Frowning, he swung the painting back to its original position, and then he called Gustavia over.

"Look, here's the spot where the light was shining before. Put your finger right there, pointing to that spot." She did, and he gently swung the painting again. Now Gustavia's finger was pointing at a different location, the scrolled trim on the center support brace between the shelves.

"Ah, I see," she said. "I'll get the others." And she left the room only to return shortly with her friends in tow. "Watch," she instructed. Then she and Tyler repeated their previous actions.

"Oh." And with not another word, the group returned to the library where Julius was still standing. This time, when Julie reached out and tentative finger, she felt a small indent in the carved trim. A gentle prod, a soft click, and what looked like a decorative panel below the shelves slid back to reveal a small recess.

As one, Tyler and Julie dropped to their knees to peer inside. They both took a look then leaned back to look at each other with identical expressions on their faces. Gustavia couldn't take it anymore. "What is it? Are you trying to kill me with suspense?"

"It's empty." Julie began to laugh, "After all this, the thing is empty."

"No; no, it isn't," Amethyst spoke in her husky voice. It wasn't precisely an aura she could see, only people and animals carried those; but items they handled with great intent sometimes carried a residual energy field that appeared to her as a faint, glowing light. And the panel was emanating that light now.

Grinning like a toddler with a cookie, Tyler pulled out his keys and, turning on the small, attached penlight, handed it to Julie who shined it into the compartment. Gustavia, leaning over her in excitement, was the first to see the shape of a tiny, tarnished silver spoon lying on the floor. Tyler reached in and pulled it out, holding it up for Kat to take it from him.

"Is that all?" Gustavia burst out.

"No." And Julie leaned into the compartment far enough to twist and look above the opening. There, hanging on a hook, was an old burlap bag, bulging at the seams. Julie slithered back out and gestured for Tyler to take her place. He reached up and lifted the heavy bag from its hidden hook, struggled to guide it carefully down to the floor, then dragged it out of its hiding place.

The contents of the bag clanged softly as Julie, with shaking hands, untied the string holding the neck of the bag closed and slowly opened it to reveal more tarnished silver inside. Her heart strained in her chest, pounding a frantic beat. She couldn't believe they'd finally found it; this whole ordeal was finally over. Throwing her head back, Julie shrieked **Woohoo!** Loud enough that everyone jumped and began laughing and talking all at once.

Amethyst cleared off the desk as Gustavia shoved Tyler out of the way so she could help Julie pull the pieces from the large, rough-textured bag. Teapots, gravy boats, platters, footed bowls, and cups appeared and were stacked on the desk, along with several pairs of heavy candlesticks.

Strangely enough, after finding the single spoon on the floor, there were no others in the bag. Gustavia noticed it first and took it upon herself to grab the penlight and crawl into the opening. Twisting her lithe body, she shined the light up into the cavity.

"Um, guys," her voice was muffled by the closeness of the space. "Here, grab this," and she dragged another bag from the small shelf that ran around the inside of the compartment and handed it out to Amethyst. Kat was there to grab the next item: a squarish packet wrapped in what looked like old tea towels and tied with string. By the time she was done, Gustavia had handed out several more bundles from inside the hiding place.

All this time, Julius stood silently next to the desk amid the faint blue glow Julie had seen the first night, the one that had begun this search. His eyes were shining, and he looked like he was about to burst; but, still, he said not a word.

Slowly, the tension in the room built as everyone realized Julius wanted to say something; but was being prevented from speaking, the frustration evident on his face. Kat, with a quiet exclamation, sank down on one of the leather chairs. Her head dropped forward as Estelle gently pulled her consciousness away and moved to stand with Julius. Gustavia perched on the arm of Kat's chair, reaching out to rub a reassuring hand across her friend's softly trembling shoulders.

"So, what happens next? Are the two of you leaving? Do you see the light?" Julie wasn't sure if she was ready to say goodbye just yet. There was not a sound in the room as Estelle gazed at her beloved granddaughter before both spirits simply faded away.

Finally alone, Tyler grabbed Julie and swung her around the kitchen several times before setting her on her feet.

"I only had time for a quick bit of research while everyone was leaving, but it looks like there's more than enough money in what we found to repair the roof and put in a security system."

Julie felt a huge sense of relief. At times during the past few weeks, she had been scared to let herself hope they would find anything and, at other times, she was afraid of what would happen when they did. She knew Tyler cared for her and she loved him, but what if it was the treasure hunt that had him interested? He was used to a certain amount of excitement in his job; and, normally, her life was pretty quiet. It wasn't like she found a lost family fortune every day of the week.

Tyler watched the play of emotions track across Julie's face and was afraid she might be having second thoughts about their relationship. It had only been a matter of weeks, but he had known she was the one for him almost since the beginning. There was no doubt on his part; he wanted to spend the rest of his life with this woman. Whether she'd found her fortune or not, whether her dead relatives never went away, whether her crazy ex came back or not, he didn't care. He loved her—

everything about her—and he intended
to show her just how much.

"Julie…"

"Tyler…"

They both spoke at once. "No, let me
go first." Tyler took Julie's hands in his
and gazed intently into her eyes until
Julie felt as though she was lost in a
sea of blue. After a moment, he shook
his head to break the spell of silence
then he spoke.

"These past few weeks have been
amazing; I can't tell you how much this
time has meant to me."

Oh, God, he's about to tell me it's
over. Her heart sank all the way into
her shoes.

He went on. "I mean, words are what I'm about; and, yet, I'm stumbling over my own tongue. I'm trying to say I love you, Julie. I know you probably think it's too soon, but I knew. Almost from the first day, I knew."

Mouth open, Julie just stared at him. He wasn't breaking up with her; he loved her. She started to laugh; it just bubbled up from so deep inside she couldn't help herself. Then she saw the look on his face and knew he was trying to figure out why she found his revelation so amusing.

"No, no. It's good, it's just I've always prided myself on not being impetuous, not being a romantic. And look where it got me. I was engaged to a cold-hearted criminal. Then I met you, and it was just... I couldn't help myself. I fell for you, right from the start. And I thought I shouldn't be sure, not this sure, not this soon. It's not normal; but, you know what, I don't care. I love you. Now and always."

He pulled her into his arms, holding her so tightly she could feel the pounding of his heart against hers—or was it hers against his? As he bent his head to kiss her, they heard a faint bell-like bonging sound followed by a clicking noise.

"Old house noises?"

"Angel getting her wings?" They both spoke at once with identical smiles on their faces.

"Now, where were we?" Tyler pulled Julie close, and they murmured words of love between soul bonding kisses until the intensity was too much to ignore and they led each other upstairs.

Epilogue

One Month Later

Tyler manned the new barbecue grill. It was the first time he had ever tried cooking veggie burgers, but he thought they looked okay. He was only a little bit nervous as he thought about the ring in his pocket, the one he planned to slip onto Julie's finger after they'd finished eating. It seemed right that all of their friends be together for the occasion. After all, they were her family.

He'd come up with any number of scenarios for proposing: just the two of them having a picnic in the gazebo, or maybe he should make a public spectacle at Wednesday night Karaoke. But, instead, he'd settled on this simple gathering that would mean the most to Julie. Once they finished eating, it would be time; and, as the meal progressed, so did the nervous feeling.

Halfway through the meal, Kat lifted her head and spoke, "It's not over."

What's not over? Julie wondered.

"We have to go to the library, now."
Tyler's heart sank; maybe this wasn't
the time for his proposal.

A look was passed between the
group, one that plainly said, "Now
what?"

But, they went inside and walked up
the stairs to find out what Kat was
talking about. There, standing behind
the desk, were both Julius and Estelle.

Time stretched. Everyone just
stared, then Julie held up both hands.
"We found the magic garden; we found
the key, and we found the hiding place.
What more is there?"

At that, Julius' eyes widened, and he
held up both hands in a gesture of

futility before pointedly looking at the panel that hid the secret area.

This time, Tyler pressed the hidden switch to open the panel.

"There must be something else to find. Gustavia, are you sure the shelf was empty?"

"I think so."

"I'm the smallest. Let me in there." Amethyst scooted past Gustavia and into the opening, then reached out a hand gesturing impatiently for Tyler to pull out his keys with the penlight. The space was about two and a half feet deep by four feet high, and cleverly built into the wall between the library and one of the bedrooms. Shelving in both rooms with decorative lower panels hid the discrepancy well enough that even Tyler's keen eyes had not noticed it when he looked at the building plans.

"I can't feel anything, and I don't see anything on the shelf," Amethyst called out, as she shifted her body to get a better look around. "Wait, there is something. Hey, someone give me a cell phone, one with a camera."

There was a scramble as they all reached for theirs at once. Julie got to hers and handed it over. Ammie twisted around to get a better angle and loosed a few choice words at the awkwardness of the movement. Before long, they all saw the flash as the camera recorded whatever she had found. After a bit more shuffling and several more flashes, she emerged from the compartment with a few cobwebs in her hair and a streak of dust across her cheek. Her eyes were glittering, though, as Tyler and Gustavia both reached down to help her up.

"You got that laptop handy?" she asked Tyler, and while he went to get it, hit the keys needed to send the images to his email. It only took a few moments for him to boot up the laptop and download the message. When the photos popped up on the screen, everyone stared for a second or two; then, as one, they all looked at Julius who gazed back at them, then shrugged his shoulders with chagrin.

"There are four keys, and we've only found the first one." Julie looked up at her grandfather who now carried the look of someone who had just been released from bondage.

"Yes, there are..." and before he could say more, Julie finished for him, "and you can't tell me anything else— don't bother, I know the drill." She crossed her arms and pinned him with a steely glare before relenting with an affectionate grin. Which he returned. "You and your friends did a fine job the first time. I know you are up to the task. You've proved that already."

Estelle chimed in, "And besides, there's Logan to consider. I'm sure we haven't heard the last of him."

Tyler spoke up, "Well, after everything, this might seem a bit anti-climactic; but since you two are here, the time feels right after all," and, turning to Julie, he took a knee.

Julie knew exactly what was about to happen; her heart raced with excitement and love as he pulled the ring from his pocket and took her hand in his.

"Julie, I love you with everything that I am or ever will be. Will you let me spend the rest of my life showing you? Will you marry me?"

Eyes shining, Julie pulled him to his feet, saying over and over, "Yes, yes, yes," as she leaped into his arms. There wasn't a dry eye in the room. Laughing and crying at once, Amethyst pulled a ten out of her pocket and passed it across to Kat saying, "I'll never learn."

The house was finally empty. After an evening of celebration and the making of plans to start figuring out the next set of clues, everyone had finally gone home leaving Julie and Tyler alone to bask in their newly engaged bliss.

Tyler had just pulled Julie into a kiss when they both heard a soft sob. With a rueful smile, Tyler rested his forehead against Julie's and whispered, "Estelle." Julie sighed. She loved her grandmother, but it was time to set some boundaries. She took a deep breath, readying herself to speak, when Tyler whispered again, "No, let me," and turned to pin Estelle with an unrelenting stare.

The seconds stretched out as Estelle began to squirm under his steady gaze. He didn't have to say a word. She finally held up both hands in surrender. "Okay, I get it. You need privacy, and I forgot to ring the doorbell. It won't happen again," her voice dropped at the end.

Tyler relented, "Thank you for being so considerate, Estelle."

Now it was her turn to stare with narrowed eyes. "It's **Grams** to you, my boy, and don't forget it. Welcome to the family. Now, I'll leave you two alone. I promise, I won't peek ever again," and with that, she was gone, for now.

The End?